ESCAPE ATTEMPT

ESCAPE ATTEMPT

MIGUEL ÁNGEL HERNÁNDEZ

Translated from the Spanish by
Rhett McNeil

Hispabooks Publishing

Hispabooks Publishing, S. L.
Madrid, Spain
www.hispabooks.com

Originally published in Spain as *Intento de escapada* by Anagrama, 2013
First published in English by Hispabooks, 2016
English translation copyright © by Rhett McNeil
Design © simonpates - www.patesy.com

ISBN 978-84-943658-7-4 (trade paperback)
ISBN 978-84-943658-8-1 (ebook)
Legal Deposit: M-157-2016

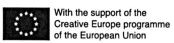 With the support of the
Creative Europe programme
of the European Union

The European Commission support for the production of this publication
does not constitute an endorsement of the contents which reflects the views
only of the authors, and the Commission cannot be held responsible for any
use which may be made of the information contained therein.

To Raquel, for everything

There are people who can be defined
by what they escape from, and people who are
defined by the fact that they are forever escaping.

ADAM PHILLIPS

Art is a dirty thing, and there is
no way to clean it without it losing its color.

JACOBO MONTES

CONTENTS

PROLOGUE

(With Hidden Noise)

I entered the room covering my mouth with a handkerchief. I could only advance a few meters. The stench was intolerable. The putrefaction penetrated every one of the pores of my skin. My stomach turned, and a bitter taste began to rise in my throat. I closed my eyes and clenched my teeth to keep down the vomit. I tried to hold my breath as long as I could. Five seconds, ten, fifteen, twenty, thirty . . . a little longer, forty, fifty . . . until the nausea subsided and my body began to get acclimated. Only then was I able to open my eyes and direct my gaze to the center of the room. And there I was able to see, at last, the box, theatrically illuminated in the midst of the darkness.

The structure, approximately one meter tall by one and a half meters wide, was made of wood and had metal reinforcements at the corners. Next to it were two small screens that played a sequence of moving images. On the first, a person entered the interior of the box. Then someone approached the box and attached the lid on top. This action was repeated on a loop. The second screen displayed the closed box. No one entered or exited from it. The wooden box simply sat there.

The same one that emanated the smell that was making my stomach turn. The same one that was right there in front of me, in that exhibition hall in the Centre Georges Pompidou in Paris. The same one that had next to it a small label on which could be read: Jacobo Montes, *Escape Attempt*, 2003.

The piece was part of the exhibition that opened the new season at the art center. *With Hidden Noise: That Which Art Conceals*, more than fifty works from the historical avant-garde to the present day, which intended to demonstrate that art is always concealing something beyond what we can see. Works that were hidden, veiled, crossed out, covered, wrapped, erased, and even destroyed. Duchamp, Manzoni, Morris, Christo, Acconci, Beuys, Richter, Salcedo . . . and at the end of the lineup, as if it couldn't have been any other way, Jacobo Montes, the great socially engaged contemporary artist.

I had gone to Paris to try to finish a book. The Ministry of Education had given me a travel grant, and my intention was to bring to a close, finally, the research that had kept me occupied for the last ten years of my life: the rupture of visual pleasure in contemporary art. I dedicated my doctoral dissertation to this issue. The majority of my writing since then never ceased to perambulate around the same problem. But it was all scattered about in short articles and essays for catalogues, and I couldn't find a way to give shape to all that material. After several years of frenetic work, the moment had arrived to bring it all together, rewrite it, and assemble the definitive version of the book. The exhibit was the perfect excuse to start fresh. And the stay in Paris would allow me to dedicate the necessary time to the matter.

I had known for some time that this exhibition was going to open in Paris. And I was able to arrange everything so that my trip would coincide with this event. The fact that a place like the Pompidou was organizing a show about concealment and occultation certified that my work on antivision continued to be relevant. The exhibit fell squarely into the field of my research. Hiding things, removing them from view, is nothing more than frustrating the spectator's gaze. To conceal, strike through, veil, enclose . . . to rupture visual pleasure.

I went to Paris to write a book. That's what I told the university. It was also what I told myself. But deep down I knew that this wasn't totally true. At least not entirely so. There was something more. Something that I clearly knew I would find in that place. Something that was now right in front of me and was making my stomach roil. Jacobo Montes, that indispensable, lauded artist, a fundamental figure of contemporary art. And his masterpiece, *Escape Attempt*, the one I had sought out so many times, the one that, ten years earlier, I hadn't had the courage to face, the one that, ever since then, never ceased to trouble me.

I wasn't alone at the exhibition. Visitors surrounded the box. They circled around it, trying to find meaning for what they saw, imagining what was inside that mysterious object, searching for a connection between

15

the videos that were playing and what was right in front of their eyes; asking themselves, for certain, if the figure who had entered the box had remained there, if the stench of decomposition they could barely stomach had something to do with this body that never revealed itself again. I know that this possibility was passing through their minds, that they might think that something didn't add up, that at bottom it was all pure contradiction, a game . . . a work of art. I intuited it, recognized the way they looked at it, understood their questions. I had asked myself those questions thousands of times. Again and again. Just like them. Because I didn't know what was inside that structure either.

But there was something that I did, indeed, know. Something other people didn't. The history of the box, its past, its origin. I knew this better than all those in the room at that moment. Better than the director of the museum, the curator of the exhibition, the art critics from specialized publications. Better than all of them. And I knew it because I'd been there. Because, sometime before, ten years earlier, I had been the privileged witness of that escape attempt.

At that moment, as I observed the visitors speculating about the thing in front of their eyes, images began to flood back into my head. And at that instant I became aware that there was something of mine inside there. Even though I was outside the box, my story remained enclosed within it. It was then that I remembered the day on which I'd heard Montes's name for the first time. The recollection came like a sharp blow. Montes. A hammer strike. A harmful explosion that pulverized my retina. Montes. A scream from within the wood.

And it all unfurled before me.

Like a fan, the past opened itself before me. The end of the 2003 term, Montes, Helena, the city, the lies, the disappointments, the fugitive impressions, the shadow, the escape attempts . . . and Omar, unfortunate Omar. Everything was there, hazy, blurry, voluntarily filed away in a corner of my memory. A dense iconostasis that kept me from distinguishing it clearly. But the vision of the box, the stench, the bitter aftertaste, the repressed vomit, the roiling stomach . . . they all combined on that afternoon to bring things to the present.

A lash from a whip opened the box of images.

And the story started to spring up in my head like an incessant noise. A hidden noise that I no longer knew how to silence.

I. FUGITIVE IMPRESSIONS

1

In the beginning was the image. The penis, in the foreground, held against a wooden board. Then, the brutal act. The hammer, the nail, and the sharp blow, which pierced the piece of flesh and secured it to the wood. The image, a flash across the screen that managed to topple me. And much later, the voice: "Those who are overly sensitive can leave the classroom." The warning, as always, after the image. First sight, which disturbs, then sound, which warns. Too late. As ever.

The image, the darkened classroom, the last visual arts course, and Helena, her voice, warning us of the rawness of the images and putting a title to the film being shown: Sick. The Life and Death of Bob Flanagan, Supermasochist. Kirby Dick. 1997.

Nailed, the Bob Flanagan performance piece that was projected onto the screen, also nailed itself to my pupils and never left that spot. The strike of the hammer pierced my retina, as it certainly did with all of my classmates. Some turned their heads away. Others even closed their eyes. No one could bear the sight of the punctured penis. And if someone's gaze remained fixed on the screen, it disappeared completely when a few small drops of blood splattered across the lens of the camera that was filming the action.

The image formed part of the film. It couldn't be understood outside of its context. And the context—the life of Bob Flanagan—the life that was revealed by these images, revealed that the artist liked pain, he took pleasure in it. It was his salvation. Facing the torment of illness—the cystic fibrosis that the artist had suffered from childhood—he resisted it with his own pain. A pain inflicted on himself, that not only gave him pleasure, but made him feel alive as well. The pain of illness smelled of death, pus, and mucus. The smell of blood, of the wound he caused, was pure vitality. When, in another fragment of the film, Flanagan's partner sliced a knife through his testicles, inserted a steel ball into his anus, or tightened a rope around his neck until she almost asphyxiated him, the artist seemed to feel liberated. And when he moaned in pleasure it shattered the surgical scene of the pretend autopsy.

The majority of people diagnosed with cystic fibrosis die before reaching the age of twenty. Flanagan lived until he was forty. And his pain, the sovereign pain, was the thing that kept him alive. At least until the end of the film. Because at the end, as if it couldn't be any other way, Flanagan was dying in a hospital, trying to escape the role of artist that he had played during a large portion of his life.

In that moment, Flanagan seemed like a miracle to me. A macabre miracle.

When the film ended, someone turned on the lights. There she was, next to the screen, leaning against the desk, Helena, dressed in black, with dark hair, long bangs, sharp profile, her forehead pale, fragile, weak, haggard, as if she were ill, as if she had escaped from one of Flanagan's performances.

With a frail, breathy voice, she said:

"Reactions?" And then she stood staring at the class, searching for a response. No one responded.

Again:

"Nothing to say?"

Just a few murmurs. Indistinguishable. Then the words came.

"Fucking crazy."

"He should have been locked up."

"Crazies are everywhere."

Everyone seemed to be in agreement. Flanagan was disturbed. He was crazy. He wasn't an artist. This film shouldn't be shown. I understood their comments. There was something in those images capable of upsetting anybody. But I intuited that there was also something that went beyond insanity. Something that was worth the effort. I could see it, it was clear to me. Which is why I decided to participate.

I outlined my argument on a piece of paper as if it were a speech, raised my hand, and started to speak, with a feeling of fear more than anything else:

"What I think," I said, "is that if the image surprises and outrages us, it's because we didn't expect it. The complete opposite of the cruel images on TV. We're used to living with those."

My classmates looked at me. Few of them shared the sentiment I was expressing. I looked at Helena. And she, for one, appeared to follow the line of argumentation. So I continued. And said that those terrible images were a basic part of our diet and that these days no one could have proper digestion without a daily session of hungry children, suffering mothers, and dismembered bodies. I said that it was possible that food wouldn't agree so well with us without this spice that serves as a condiment for our food. Salt, oil, vinegar, and, of course, blood, guts, arms, legs, and sobs. We must find some inner satisfaction in these images if we continue watching them, if we keep eating as if it were nothing, and we don't take up arms and go out and start shooting at people in the streets in order to set things aright.

My participation in class made me emotional. And though I already wanted to stop, I couldn't find a way to do it. It's always taken a lot of work for me to start talking, but often it is even more difficult to stop.

"I don't believe that we are blinded by images and that we can no longer see anything," I continued. "It isn't the media that's deceiving us. We're the guilty ones, the ones who, deep down, want to eat with these images in the background. We're vampires who take pleasure in blood, and it only seems like our existence makes any sense when we know that the other is a fucking piece of shit and is constantly being blown to bits. The screen is what saves us. And sometimes we pretend that we're moved by what we see. But we aren't the least fucking bit moved. Sometimes we even shed a tear. And the tear falls into our soup, and then we start eating again, and we notice that the soup is even more delicious, and that our tears make everything taste better. But it's not our tears. It's the blood of the other, the blood spilled. This is what truly makes it salty. This is what seasons it. Our tears are fucking shit next to this blood seasoning."

After saying all this I felt exhausted, as if I had pulled something out of myself that had been in there for quite a while. No one said a word. Someone snorted. People looked down at their desks. A few short seconds of silence. Eternal seconds. And only after these ended did Helena thank me for my participation.

The remaining lights were turned on—before that we had been sitting in a half-light—and I began collecting my notes. In the midst of that minor racket, I again heard Helena's voice.

"Just a minute," she said. "Tomorrow is the last day of class for this course. We'll end the course with the work of Jacobo Montes. If Bob Flanagan was hard for you to take, I don't know what terms you'll employ to describe the work of Montes."

Jacobo Montes. It was the first time I'd ever heard this name.

I didn't yet know that I would never be able to get it out of my head.

2

"I've come to remind you of something you already know and that, this time, you won't be able to escape," said the feminine voice through the intercom.

I immediately recognized Sonia and guessed what she had come to remind me about, although I wasn't sure whether I wanted to escape from it or not. The exam period was to commence the following week, and we had to celebrate the last night of partying before we shut ourselves off from the world.

"How are you, Marcos? And the others?" she asked after entering and sitting down on the couch in the living room, crossing her legs as if she were a Hollywood actress.

"Don't know and don't care," I replied. And it was true. The "others" were my roommates. And even though I lived with them, it was basically like I lived alone. I knew little more about their lives than their names, that one was studying Spanish and another was trying to finish a degree in geography. I didn't need any more information. That was enough for me. I'd come to an agreement with them. I lived there. There were common spaces. And sometimes we even crossed paths in the hallway. That was it. Nothing more was needed.

The only thing that mattered to me at that point was that they left me in peace and didn't interrupt me when I lowered the blinds in my room and shut myself in to read, listen to music, watch movies on my computer, or think as I lay on my bed. That they didn't interrupt me under any circumstances. Because this was truly what I had sought in that apartment, far from my hometown, from my mother's constant interruptions, from my neighbors' prying eyes, and the sort of interior hallway that my street had become.

What is still not very clear to me is why I allowed Sonia to interrupt me. I think about it now and the only thing that occurs to me is that it was because she was the only one who knew when she was bothering me. And she didn't mind leaving at those moments. Perhaps for this reason our friendship was established, because she perceived what no one else had ever known about me: the moments when I needed to be alone. But she also sensed—and I still don't know how she did it—those moments when you say that you don't want to do something, but deep down you're thinking the opposite. Those moments when, without quite knowing why, you don't do something despite the fact that you have the desire to do it. And I had a lot of those moments. Nevertheless, on that night it was totally clear to me that I didn't want to go out partying the next day. So I told her that it would be better to leave it for some other time.

"Don't even say it. This Thursday you're not leaving me by myself. Even if I have to drag you out of your bedroom. Look at you, your face has lost all its color."

"Sonia, I really don't want to. I've already told you this a bunch of times. It's not my thing. I don't like the music they play at those places, alcohol makes me feel awful, and the next day my body is just useless."

"But you'll start cracking jokes and end up having a good time."

"That's a lie. You know it. I feel uncomfortable. Besides, there's the whole issue of . . . girls. I'm already somewhat sick of going out and then coming home feeling jealous."

"This is the thing I don't understand."

"What don't you understand?"

"That you don't hook up with anyone. With that good-little-boy face of yours . . ." she said, pinching my cheeks.

"Yeah, very adorable. Have you taken a good look at me?" And for a moment I observed my body from the outside. Since I was little my mother had told me that I was as pretty as a girl and that I looked like one of Salzillo's angels. But when you grow into adolescence with that same face and not much taller, and then add to that a hundred kilos of bodyweight, rapidly worsening nearsightedness, and incipient balding, the situation is different. And when, on top of that, you always wear black—convinced that it makes you look slimmer—and shirts that are two sizes too big so that your spare tire doesn't show, the image projected isn't exactly that of a seducer. For that reason, at the age of twenty-two, I was still a virgin and convinced that the nightlife wasn't for me.

"Gimme a break, don't complain. To my mind, you're not that bad."

"You're just saying that because you're . . ."

"What? A dyke?" she retorted, without letting me finish. And I immediately realized that I had put my foot in my mouth. For some reason Sonia didn't really like to be reminded of it. Very few people knew; even some of her close friends didn't know. And her mother still bragged at church about her beautiful single daughter.

"I was going to say . . . because you're my friend." I put emphasis on the last word, knowing that I was lying.

"It doesn't matter. We all have problems of some sort. Things aren't always easy."

"I'm sorry, forgive me, truly."

"Well, about Thursday . . . you already know. Even if I have to bring the whole gay brigade, I'm getting you out of here."

"You win," I ended up saying, resigned. Sonia gave me a kiss on the cheek and then looked at me for a few seconds.

"By the way—to change the subject—you finished today, right?"

"Tomorrow. All that's left is my last contemporary art class."

"You're taking Helena, right? You're so fucking lucky. I ended up with the incompetent Navarro. That guy is such a dumbass."

"I know. I suffered through him freshman year. Helena is something else. Today we saw some images that left me stunned. Have you heard of Bob Flanagan?"

Sonia shook her head.

"Want to see something outrageous?"

We went into my bedroom and sat down in front of the computer. I searched the internet for pictures of Flanagan and showed her.

"That's rough stuff," she said upon seeing Flanagan's punctured penis. "Why is everyone so crazy?"

"Well, you have to see it in its context." I didn't feel like I had the strength to argue much more than that.

I tried to find a video of Flanagan's performance, but the majority of them seemed to be censored. I only found the last part of the film, which showed Flanagan's death in the hospital. Since there was no explicit sex or violence in it, the scene was circulating around the internet with no problems. It's odd, for me those were the most awful images. And they were for Sonia, too, who, after only watching for a few seconds, had a different expression on her face.

"I think I've seen too much. I don't feel like watching any more of this right now."

I then recalled something that I clearly should have realized before I ever showed her anything. Sonia's father had spent the entire year in the hospital with lung cancer and, even though the tumor now seemed to have subsided, it was understandable that she still might be sensitive about hospitals.

"I'll close this immediately, don't worry."

"Doesn't matter, actually, I'm gonna go, it's already getting late. Plus, I don't want to distract you any longer."

"Your call."

"See you tomorrow. Get to bed soon and get ready for some partying tomorrow."

She gave me a hug and left the bedroom as if she were in her own home. From a distance, I heard the door shut.

I remained in the shadows of the bedroom, surrounded by bare walls on which there wasn't a single drawing, a single painting, a single poster. Just books and more books, as if, instead of a supposed aspiring artist, a literature student were living there. I sometimes asked myself why I ended up studying visual arts. And I couldn't find the answer. I liked images, interpreting them, understanding them, but not producing them. There were already too many of them in the world to keep on adding more.

I leaned back on the bed, rested the laptop on my legs, and started to watch the final sequence of *Sick*. As had happened during class, what I saw once again moved me.

Death is, without a doubt, the most radical gesture made by an artist. Flanagan had achieved the ultimate work of art. The artist, exhibiting his illness and his own death. Many others had worked with death and illness. But none of them had attained true death, as Flanagan had. None of them had been able to exhibit themselves as a corpse.

In the film you see Flanagan pass away. You can clearly see when the face of death falls upon him. That's the cruelest moment. Not the punctured penis, not the perforated nipples, not the wounds, not the shit, not the urine, not the blood. Nothing was more terrible than the agonized face of the artist. Everything was happening there. A true, absolute piety.

31

In the darkness of my bedroom, that night I watched Flanagan in his hospital bed and, at his side, his partner, Sheree Rose. And I noticed that in these moments Flanagan no longer represented anything. He was merely a body. A body that, for the first time, didn't care about the camera. He was no longer acting, not even for himself. For the first time, his pain was real, completely real, without partition, without distance, without leaving any part—ever smaller, yet always present—to the spectator.

That night it became clear to me that Flanagan wasn't pretending. But I couldn't say the same for his partner. She was pure fiction, she was the representation that was needed to keep the scene together. She was the dramatic element that made it able to be understood as a work of art. I sensed it. For some reason, I knew it: she had been faking it from the beginning. She was faking it while Flanagan was dying. She was faking it at the burial. And she was faking it afterwards, when she showed the camera what remained of the artist, his pus and snot, the remnants she had decided to keep, like some abject shrine.

Yes, she was pretending. He, however, wasn't capable of it. And that night I thought that perhaps she was the true artist. Because the artist is always faking it. The artist is a subject. And subjects fake it. Flanagan, however, had transformed himself into an object, into Rose's material. And for that reason he ceased to be an artist. Because an object can't be an artist. Perhaps, then, Flanagan was a work of art. The object, the material, the form. And Rose, the artist. Or maybe not. Maybe Flanagan was at once both subject and object, artist and artwork, just like a prostitute, who is merchant and merchandise, subject and object, will and stone, all at once. But the prostitute doesn't get worn out, or gets less worn out. Flanagan wore himself out, indeed. Or, on second thought, prostitutes also get worn out. But Flanagan's object was already worn out. Or, better said, he was the subject that had worn himself out. He had worn himself out and transformed himself into an object. An abject corpse. The ultimate work of art. Life as a work of art. And death, above all, death, the final frontier, the border past which no one had yet dared to cross. The border that Flanagan opened up. Or maybe he hadn't opened up anything, maybe it was all just a failed attempt, and maybe there was no art in it at all. Or maybe, at bottom, it had just gotten way too late and my head was no longer good for anything. Which is why I turned off the computer and put it on my nightstand.

Only later, when I was half-asleep, did I remember Montes. I'd forgotten to look up information about him on the internet. It would have been nice to take a quick peek at his work before class the next day. But it was already very late. I'd started to doze off and didn't want to move from where I was. No matter. Montes could wait. Dreaming was more important.

3

The images flashed across the screen at a dizzying rhythm. I only had time to observe the presence of some hooks, two or three hanging bodies, and some blood on the ground.

"Don't worry, this will all make sense in a moment," said Helena while she checked to make sure her presentation was in order and all the videos were working correctly. I gave a slight nod of agreement and finished drinking the coffee that I'd just bought from the vending machine.

On Thursdays, I arrived to class early in order to avoid the traffic jams on the roads into campus. This allowed me to watch Helena's ritual. The same one had been repeated throughout the entire course, always identical, as if she were following some sort of pattern that I wasn't able to discern. Fifteen minutes before class, dressed in black, she would enter the classroom with her leather briefcase and timidly wave hello to me, remove her laptop, set it on the desk, and connect it to the projector; once she had made certain that everything was working, she went through the images she was going to show in class one by one, comparing them with what she had written down in her notes, as if she had to study them all again, examining her pages over and over.

It was curious that her apparent insecurity disappeared entirely when she began to speak in class. Because at that moment, her whispered, fragile voice—which, since the very first day of class, had reminded me of Najwa Nimri's in *Abre los ojos*—seemed assured, firm, forceful, as if everything she said weren't something read and learned, but lived and experienced, as if she truly believed in the power of the images she showed us.

And there was something to this. Because the truth was that Helena had a lot of experience in the real world. That course was the only one she taught at the university. The rest of the time she worked as the director of one of the art galleries in the city. So she had an inside knowledge of the art world, not like the rest of the professors, whose knowledge of art came from what they'd read in books. And, for some of them, not even that.

Helena was the only one worth a damn in that department. And I couldn't help but observe her with absolute fascination. Despite her youth—she wasn't yet even thirty-five years old—she knew so much more than I ever thought I could possibly know. She had traveled to countries and places I could only dream of. She had met artists I admired. She had lived through things I couldn't even imagine—and about which I sometimes fantasized. Because of this, I sometimes wondered why she stayed in that provincial city and hadn't moved back to the capital, or moved abroad, or to any other place outside that city, which, without a doubt, must have seemed small to her.

After the ten minute grace period was up, Helena turned off the lights and started her class in the darkness:

"I didn't want to end this course without you all seeing the work of Jacobo Montes, who is, as I see it, the most important, brilliant, and controversial Spanish creator of recent years. An artist, nevertheless, who has gone unnoticed by a large portion of the art critics in this country. Perhaps for that reason you haven't heard much about him, even though, for some time now, his work has received constant attention on the international stage, especially because his evolution, in a certain way, sums up the itineraries of the most progressive art trends from the 80s and is today reaching its crucial moment of maturity and recognition."

I adjusted my pen and papers, and prepared myself to take notes. The moment had arrived to find out who Montes was.

Helena began talking about the artist's origins and told us that, even though he was born in Madrid, he had been educated in the United States, where he still resided. There, during the 80s, he was fully involved with the activist movement in which art was transformed into a tool for demanding rights, a political weapon of the highest order. But his beginnings are to be found in his relationship with a group of Californian artists who would later be known as the "Modern Primitives."

While she said this, the images I'd caught glimpses of before class appeared on the screen. A naked man piercing his nipples with hooks that were attached to a tree with wires. Then, he started to move around the tree and the skin of his chest began to stretch little by little, until it reached a point where it seemed that it was going to be ripped off in shreds. The image reminded me of a scene from a Western that I'd watched with my father years earlier.

"What you're seeing," said Helena, "is an emulation of the 'Dances of the Sun' practiced by many primitive tribes as a central part of a ritual of knowledge. Fakir Musafar, whom you see here with a sword pierced through his face"—another image appeared on the screen—"was one of the most important figures in the introduction of these practices into the artistic realm. A former Silicon Valley executive who, tired of his comfortable life, began to search for spiritual elevation through the mortification of his body, emulating some of the techniques of Eastern fakirs."

Helena projected some more images of suspensions. People with hooks pierced through them, hung from trees and platforms, performances and large events where the elevations where performed by a group. A sort of grand baptism of blood and weightlessness.

"What this is about, at bottom," she continued, "is lifting the feet off the ground, levitating, but this time in a real, physical manner. This has been one of the obsessions of artists during modernity, spiritual elevation. And some of them have achieved it, or at least have sought after it, through physical elevation, through a battle waged against the force of gravity. From Malevich, with his paintings of airplanes, to the levitations of the magician David Blaine, or from the suspensions of Francesca Woodman to the physical feat of Philippe

Petit on a wire between the Twin Towers. To fly, to elevate oneself, to escape . . . to leave this world that holds us fast to the earth and keeps our head just above the ground."

Helena was speaking of elevation, thus delaying the appearance of Montes. I started to get anxious. Where was he? Was it that there were no images of his work? For a moment I even started to think that maybe his name had just been bait to ensnare our attention. But this thought quickly vanished.

A naked body, wrapped in a tangle of cables and ropes, hung from a rafter, slightly elevated from the ground. Underneath his feet was a small puddle of blood. You could barely see his face.

"This is Montes," Helena finally proclaimed. "In the early 80s, he began to perform suspensions, inspired by Musafar, and soon entered into contact with Flanagan. It was during this time that he became interested in masochism as an instrument for understanding the world. Which is what occurs, for example, in one of his most celebrated works: *Dialectic of Illuminism*."

In the image, a woman dressed in leather inserts a series of candles into Montes's anus, each of them with the approximate diameter of a coin. The size of all of them together was larger than a human head. Within a few seconds, the anus begins to bleed. And after the first blood drips to the ground, the dominatrix lights the candles, which burn down until they begin to scorch the buttocks of the artist, whose face remains emotionless all the while. His mouth, gagged with a leather ball, emits only a faint groan.

"As you can see, the question of emptiness and illumination is addressed by Montes in a literal and physical manner. Certain forms of masochism cannot be explained entirely without allusion to central questions of philosophy. Here, without a doubt, it is easy to spot a corporeal critique of the famous *Kant avec Sade* by Jacques Lacan."

Helena spoke with complete disaffection, as if she were describing a minimalist sculpture. According to her, Montes had created these sorts of works until the end of the 80s, when he began to realize that these actions were, at bottom, solipsistic, a form of masturbation. They gave him pleasure and knowledge, but were of little use to anyone else.

At this point I overheard the commentary of my classmates at the desk behind me:

"Just like I told you, mental masturbation."

Helena didn't seem to hear anything and proceeded with her lecture:

"In time, Montes started to distance himself from this type of art in order to immerse himself in an artistic practice with greater social engagement. And little by little, he began to create art that was designed to move consciences, not for the mere act of provocation, but with the intention of making the injustices of the world visible. Since then, he has settled into a species of brutal realism that some have called "visceral sociologism."

The image on the screen changed, and a photograph of a dead dog appeared.

"During the 90s, Montes carried out actions that presented themselves as uncomfortable situations. In one of his most controversial artistic interventions—

later reworked by a few different artists—he kept a stray dog tied up for a week in front of a wall on which he had written, in dog food, the word 'hunger.' The animal died, fittingly, of hunger. None of the visitors to the gallery dared to untie him."

The murmurings in the classroom then grew louder. This time Helena heard the noise and asked what was going on. I looked at the desk behind me to ask them to be quiet, but before I could say a word, I heard the voice of one of my classmates:

"Okay, that's enough already. This whole business of people slicing up their body parts or stuffing candles up their ass, that's fine. It's for crazy people, but they aren't doing anyone any harm. To me, that's not art—far from it, in fact—but they can do what they want. But this is something else entirely. This is an outrage. It's sadism, it's abuse. It's illegal and immoral."

"And since when does art have to be good, moral, or legal?" asked Helena, not bothered in the least. "That something is a work of art does not impede it from being an evil action. For a long time now, ethics and aesthetics have been different things."

"Are you telling me that the artist is free to abuse and mistreat?"

"I'm telling you that the artist can be a son of a bitch."

Those words sounded harsh and strange in the mouth of Helena, who spoke them impassively, leaning on the desk next to the projector.

"So, by that logic, the artist could be a terrorist," said my classmate sarcastically.

"I don't see why not."

"Because a terrorist is a murderer."

"And an artist can also be one," she replied. "The history of art is full of examples."

"Maybe so. But what I'm saying is that if a person kills someone or abuses an animal, that's illegal and cannot be a work of art."

"Art and ethics are two different things," insisted Helena. "Something can be a great work of art and still be ethically abominable."

"Okay, so you say. Whatever you think. I believe that this is madness and that it should be prohibited immediately."

Helena took a deep breath. She seemed to know that she wasn't going to be able to convince him of anything. And she ended up saying:

"That's your opinion. And I don't expect to change it. I'm not here to tell you what is good and what is evil, rather only to show you the art that is created in the present day. You all are free to accept it or reject it. For me, personally, Montes's art is compelling."

Compelling, I thought. Yes. Maybe that was the word. The images of the dog had been compelling to me. But it wasn't totally clear to me what I thought about them. I understood the action itself perfectly, but I didn't know how to react.

"Think about it a little bit," said Helena, returning to the question at hand, this time with a more assertive tone. "Who is responsible for the death of the animal: the artist or the spectator?"

No one answered. Helena repeated the question. The same silence. Then she looked at me as if she were hoping for a supportive argument from a co-conspirator.

And I had no other choice but to raise my voice once more:

"The spectator, of course," I ended up saying. "If the dog finally dies, it's because no one decided to free it, because they all just looked away, trusting that someone else would come along later and be the one to shoulder the responsibility. Like the saying goes: Wait for someone, it'll never get done."

"Ergo . . . the work is effective," commented Helena. "And the dog dying is what makes it effective."

Again I heard some snickering coming from behind me. Helena looked at her watch and seemed to sense that there wasn't enough time left in class. I noticed a certain discomfort in her. Or perhaps it was frustration. Probably the frustration of knowing that, whatever she might say, she wasn't going to convince anyone. She sighed, looked at her papers, and continued the lecture.

"From this piece—the one with the dog—onward, Montes's work starts to revolve around a concept that remains central to his work and characterizes his most recent performances, something he calls the logic of reproduction. According to him, the artist is not innocent. No one is. The artist is an integral part of that which he denounces. And can only reproduce it. As such, the artist cannot come out with clean hands. Rather, he has to take part in it. Get his hands dirty, fill them with shit, as he once wrote. He often goes back to the famous phrase that Dan Flavin used to legitimize the cleanliness of minimalist art: 'I don't want to get my hands dirty.' And Montes responds: 'But your hands are filled with shit, and for as much as you try to wash them, they'll always smell of rot, wherever you are.'

This scatological metaphor, this being up to your neck in shit, is the key to his most recent works, even though, as many have argued, this is nothing new in his art. From the start, Montes has worked with the real body and the poetics of abjection. Blood, semen, urine, feces . . . but reworked on a societal level. It is the abjection of what he calls the communal body. These ideas are the key to *Immigrant's Shit*, one of Montes's most recent works. In a clear homage to Piero Mazoni and his *Merda d'artista*, Montes invited a group of immigrants to eat their own shit. At the same time, he opened one of the cans of Manzoni's excrement, bought specially for the performance for a large sum of money, and ate its contents."

The images showed a series of people seated around a large table. All of them were eating, as could be deduced from the lecture, excrement. The scene was extraordinarily unpleasant. A sort of nauseating Last Supper in which the artist ate the sacred shit, the shit that didn't stink and was literally worth its weight in gold, while the immigrants ate their own shit: hot, fetid, revolting, repulsive.

"As you can see," said Helena, "Montes is also in dialogue with the imaginary of *Saló or the 120 days of Sodom*, the Pasolini film. Nevertheless, here the torture is no longer apparent. No one is forcing anyone to do anything. The immigrants have chosen to be there. They're getting paid. Their will has been bought. And this buying of the will of another is the issue that Montes is currently working with, denouncing situations of invisibility and injustice, but not with the clean, immaculate hand of the engaged artist, rather, he causes those situations, reproduces them, making apparent that which no one wants to see."

While Helena spoke, the images became increasingly repugnant and showed an immigrant vomiting onto the plate and trying to eat his own vomit. The expressions of disgust and repulsion on the faces of the diners produced incipient feelings of nausea in me as well, which, fortunately, I managed to control.

Helena again glanced at her watch, realized that the class time had already ended, and turned on the lights at once. I squinted to accustom my eyes to the light. And for a moment I felt like I was awaking from a nightmare that was horrible, yet somehow absolutely fascinating.

"With that we have reached the end of our class and the course," concluded Helena. "You already know that the photocopies of the materials for the exam are in lecture room two and that there will be four slides, out of which you should choose three. Just one more thing," she added after a brief pause. "For those who might be interested, Jacobo Montes is mounting an exhibition here in town at the beginning of September. And you may encounter him in a few days on the streets of your neighborhood, documenting them for his work."

My eyes opened as wide as they could go, as if I'd heard something unimaginable. Montes? Here in town? It wasn't possible. Must have been a mistake. But Helena had said it. And I'd heard it perfectly.

It was the first time in the course of my studies that an artist had made me think. The first time that I didn't have any idea where I stood. What I'd seen seemed insane to me, but at the same time I felt an attraction that I couldn't control. Montes's arguments seduced me, the contradiction fascinated me. I wanted to know more. If Montes was going to come to town, I wanted to see him, wanted to meet him, or, at least, I didn't want to miss out on what he was going to do. As such, before leaving the classroom, I stopped for a moment in front of Helena's desk and asked her:

"Is it true? Jacobo Montes is putting on an exhibition here?"

"That's what I said," she replied.

I lacked the words to go on. In truth, that's what she had said. Hadn't I heard her? Asking her about it again made me seem quite awkward. But I didn't know what else to say.

"By the way," she commented, rescuing me from my silence, "what you said last class about images and the context in which we see them struck me as really intelligent."

"It's what I think. Sometimes we see things out of context, and then that's precisely when we realize what they really are. For me, art is a way to remove things from their context."

"An unhinging. *Time is out of joint*," she said in perfect English. "The artist is the one who makes us see it."

"Yeah. I believe that art has to upset and rattle the spectators. To wake them up. Because we're all asleep."

"Well, you seem to be wide awake."

"I don't know, we're all sleeping and sometimes we believe that we wake up and see something, and perhaps we don't see anything at all and keep on sleeping. And it all continues to be an illusion."

45

Helena just looked at me for a moment, as if she, too, didn't know what to say. And I thought that perhaps I had started to get confused. Sometimes I'd blurt out things like that, and I never quite knew if it was the appropriate moment to say them. So, before continuing further down that path, I changed my tone of voice and said:

"Really, the only thing I wanted to tell you was that I'm very happy that an artist like Montes is coming to our city. And that I hope that his work is able to shake up this sleepy backwater."

Then I said goodbye and made to leave the classroom. But right before I walked out the door, I heard Helena once more:

"Marcos . . . do you have a car?"

I turned around in surprise. I had my dad's Renault Laguna with me in the city. I nodded, looking at Helena.

"I'm thinking . . . Would you like to meet Montes?"

"What?"

"He's coming next week to make preparations for his piece. And he told me he'll need an assistant who can drive. It's unpaid work, but perhaps it could count towards internship credit for you. What do you think?"

"I don't know . . ." I was unsure for a moment, but then quickly decided. "I'd love to, of course. But I don't know how I might be of help."

"Don't worry. It's nothing complicated. He'll need someone who knows the city, who drives, who can help him with materials and practical concerns of that sort. And besides, I'll be around, too."

"In that case, you can count on me."

"Perfect, then. And one more thing . . . Please don't call me by the formal *usted* anymore. You're making me feel old. And I'm still in my thirties."

"Sure. So, *usted* . . . *tú*, you," I said, smiling timidly, "you'll let me know what I need to do."

As I said this, I felt that distances had been cut short by millions of kilometers, that obstacles had been lifted, and that, really, she wasn't that much older than I was, that fifteen years were almost nothing and that perhaps there was a remote possibility of something. Possibility of what? I couldn't yet imagine.

4

Montes had turned my stomach. It was the first time that had happened to me. His art had left something stuck inside me, I could feel it, like a virus that only takes effect little by little, but the presence of which is felt from the first instant. The images I'd seen in that class, and the ones I saw later when I did a little more research into his work, were lodged so deep within me that I couldn't yank them out. But it wasn't just the images. In fact, the images were the least of it. There was something more. It was the sensation of being unsure about everything, of being absolutely confused and not knowing how to act in the face of what was right in front of my eyes.

Montes had troubled me. His work had made an impact on me. And that was what art was to me then, the impact, the capacity to shake up everything. What Montes did, his way of exploiting and torturing the defenseless, turned out to be very difficult for me to come to terms with. And, however, it attracted me, intrigued me, and seduced me, like some sort of hypnosis, during which you're aware of the fact that the hypnotist is manipulating you, but still you play along because you don't know where it might take you.

Hypnotized. That was the word. Even though the hypnosis hadn't entirely convinced me. So, I wanted to know more. To know everything. To come to terms with it. To understand how that could be art, what passed through the mind of someone who treated another human being that way, and, above all, what passed through the mind of all those who, like me at that moment, were bewitched by something that was, a priori, terrifying.

That same morning, I searched the library for all the books in which I thought it might be possible to find something about Montes. There were just five textbooks on contemporary art that devoted a few final pages to him. Very little, but it was something.

When I got home, I quickly wolfed down the first thing I found in the fridge and went to cloister myself in my bedroom, the books under my arm. Right before I made it to the door, I ran into one of my housemates in the hallway as he came out of the bathroom.

"What's up, man? I'm gonna get a nap in, 'cause tonight is gonna be a long one," he said. Of course he, too—just like half the university—was planning to go out partying that night to celebrate the fact that we wouldn't be able to do it again during the next month of exams. "You're going out, too, right?"

"Yeah, of course," I replied. And then quickly shut myself in my room without another word, hoping that time would stand still so that I could disappear for a few days and concentrate on the images with which I had already started to become obsessed.

I liked to isolate myself. And when something interested me, as the art of Montes did at that moment, I couldn't wait to drop everything and lock myself in my room. More than once I'd come racing in from the street and shut myself in there as if I were running from something. Sonia was convinced that it was an illness. Reader's incontinence, she called it. And she sort of had a point. At times, I found the need to concentrate on my own things and I couldn't wait at all. When I felt like doing something, I had to do it immediately and in solitude. And most importantly, I had to have at my disposal all the time in the world, without any obligations on the horizon. The mere thought that my concentration might be interrupted at some point shot to hell the hypothetical possibility of being able to dedicate hours and hours to a single objective.

Reading, watching, and listening were to me, at least back then, actions of total immersion and isolation. I knew when I was going to open a book, but not when I was going to close it. Sometimes I'd submerge myself in the reading of a novel and wouldn't leave my room until I was able to finish it. It was obsessive behavior. But I was convinced that when you give yourself over to a work of art, you have to give it the amount of time that the work itself requires, and the world has to put on the brakes for hours, days, weeks, or even months. Over the years, I've begun to realize that this was nothing more than an adolescent utopia, that you can't disappear all that easily, and that those escapes and immersions have to be something more like quick dips and intermittences. But back then I wanted to have all the time in the world. And I naïvely believed that I could escape the vertiginous rush and rhythm of the rest of humanity.

As such, when I entered my room to immerse myself in Montes's work, knowing that in a few short hours I'd have to leave to celebrate something that made absolutely no sense to me, I couldn't help but feel a sense of sorrow that I was unable to shake throughout the whole night.

In any case, I took advantage of the time I had and read, almost in one sitting, all the material that I'd brought from the library. It wasn't a lot, and the references to Montes's work merely consisted of the final chapters of the books. So I resorted to the internet, and there it was a different story. The amount of references was practically endless: interviews, reviews of his work, notes about openings, critical appreciations, catalogue forewords . . . a whole sea of texts and images, enough to shipwreck anyone.

Upon comparing what was in the books with what was online, I realized that the present day was no longer on paper, but rather on the screen. Contemporary art is a contemporary of the digital world, and that is where you have to find it. The problem is that all the information was scattered everywhere and was, at times, contradictory. One had to assemble the text oneself, as if one were a DJ, arranging the pages in proper order, cutting, pasting, restructuring it all. Knowing has become, more than ever, an act of montage.

I started to save the most relevant pages, cutting bits of text and images and pasting them into a Word document in order to organize it all in my head. That's what I started working on that afternoon, putting it all aside for some other time, organizing it in order to give it a careful reading later on. I didn't even want to pay close attention to the images I was finding. I didn't have time. I knew that I'd soon be interrupted so I preferred not to look too closely. I was certain that if I immersed myself in this information, I wouldn't be able to escape it, they'd have to drag me out of my room kicking and screaming. So I resisted the temptation as much as I could. And even then, I couldn't help but focus on a few images that still demanded my attention no matter how much I tried to avert my eyes.

Even after I closed my laptop, I still had a series of photos branded on my retina. In it, Montes was shown on a tightrope walker's wire, first walking, then jumping, and then, later, falling onto the cable with his legs spread open. The artist's bruised testicles and the blood and flesh that remained on the wire afterwards were stuck in my head the entire night.

5

"You want it with whiskey or rum?" asked Sonia. "You just have to get a little buzz going early to take the edge off. Then you'll just go with the flow, and then it's on."

The problem was that I didn't like to just go with the flow. And, what was more, back then I also couldn't get buzzed without getting an upset stomach. Things have changed a lot since then, but in my fifth year of college—even though this might seem like science fiction—I was also practically a virgin when it came to drunken nights out. My years at university weren't exactly filled with drugs, sex, and alcohol. And that night wasn't going to be any different. At least I didn't intend on it being any different. So I told Sonia that, if she would be so kind, I'd like my Coca-Cola without alcohol.

"Okay, whatever you want, but don't start glaring at me with a look of boredom on your face."

Boredom? That wasn't exactly what I felt, more like irritation. Irritation at what was starting to take place all around me. The fact was that I couldn't stand it when the house was turned into an improvised nightclub and filled up with people I didn't know. In addition to my housemates, their friends, girlfriends, and girlfriends' friends had all come over that night, as well as a random classmate here and there who had decided to join the festivities. And they all acted like they had the right to strut right into the bedrooms and roam around the house as if they were at home. I couldn't stand the fact that I'd had to set aside Montes's art to pretend like I was having fun among all these people. I was aware that it was sometimes necessary to make concessions. But these kinds of concessions wore my patience thin. It pained me to listen to music I hated, laugh at jokes I didn't understand, and repeat over twenty times that I didn't want to try that thing that looked like some sort of mint salad with a splash of rum they insisted on calling a mojito.

Fortunately, a couple of hours later the alcohol had run low and the time to go out had arrived. And, also fortunately, the various groups divided up and I was left alone with Sonia. It was almost one in the morning and we were heading to a bar that some friends of hers owned in the neighborhood near campus. Soon after, we moved to the next bar over. And then again about a dozen more times. I was just tagging along. I had to. But I couldn't stop wondering what exactly we were looking for in bar after bar. And just like the other times I'd gone out partying—three or four, no more than that, I believe—after the whole pilgrimage had been made, when everything else was closed, Sonia ended up saying:

"Last call at El Rrose?"

El Rrose Sélavy was a gay bar that, over time, had become the place to have one final drink before heading to bed, whether alone or with a group. An *antro*, a squalid dive that you agreed to accept the moment you touched the door.

"Sure, one last drink," I said in agreement. And I did so precisely because I didn't find El Rrose Sélavy altogether unpleasant. You could barely hear the music inside, it was three streets away from my apartment, and, above all else, I had always found it intriguing that a bar would have such a Duchampian name. Further, my role as distant observer could be satisfyingly performed there better than anywhere else. On more than one occasion, as I looked around me, I smiled thinking of the double meaning of the word *antro*-pology.

We weren't surprised to find Navarro, the director of the Art Institute, there. He was leaning against a corner of the bar, dressed up like a modern, independent youth: bald and paunchy, but wearing torn jeans and a deliberately faded shirt.

Navarro had been my professor during my first year of college. The only thing I remember about his classes was that he made us attend all the conferences he organized at the Institute and that he would go on and on about how important all the professors and critics who came to give lectures and seminars were. I later found out that most of them were friends of his who, in turn, would invite him to give lectures at conferences and write essays for exhibition catalogues.

The few times I'd gone out barhopping, I always saw him out some place with an invited guest. And

Sonia said that she saw him out at the bars night after night. Depending on the sexual preference of the guest, he'd take them out to one place or another. He swung both ways, so there was never any problem.

That week the Institute had organized a conference about contemporary Spanish painting. So I assumed that the tall, well-dressed man beside him was his invited guest speaker. I knew of him because he had written one of the textbooks we had studied, an introduction to contemporary art that, looking back on it, was absolutely deplorable, even though it is still considered a crucial reference work for many. What I couldn't understand at all was how he'd allowed himself to be seduced by Navarro, first of all, to travel to this provincial town and, second, to step down from his pedestal and lower himself into such a hellish nightscape.

"Hey maaaan . . ." said Navarro as soon as he saw us, opening his arms wide, as if he wanted to hug us.

We had saved him. I knew that he loved to make himself look important. And, with us there, he could brag about his guest in front of his students and brag about his students in front of his guest. We were the perfect combination. Plus, Sonia was there, and Navarro harbored a special predilection for her.

We started to walk over to him and waved hello with an air of resignation. And just before we got to him, he started to say:

"Well look who's here, I was just explaining that my students have read all of Professor Duran's books, and then you guys show up to confirm it. Come on Marcos, tell him yourself that it's true, he doesn't believe me."

"Yes, it's true," I replied while shaking his hand. "Of course, it's a central work," I added to make a good impression.

"What a shame that you all missed the conference. It was masterful."

"Well, not so very much, not so much," said the critic, playing down Navarro's words.

"But fate, which is still showering its favor upon us, has decided we should run into each other tonight," said Navarro sarcastically.

For almost an hour we tried to tolerate the conversation. It felt like an eternity to me. Navarro wouldn't stop talking about his plans and theories, and the critic was barely paying any attention at all to him, moving his head from side to side, looking around as if searching for something to do that was actually interesting.

At some point, probably in an attempt to shut up Navarro for a second, the critic asked about our interests. Sonia told him that she wanted to graduate as soon as possible so she could take some civil service exam or another, and I told him that I'd like to write a doctoral dissertation and research contemporary art.

"A shame," interrupted Navarro. "This guy's a good student, but in this city he'll go his whole life without seeing a decent exhibition."

Then Navarro went on to say that nothing in that whole city was worth a damn and that the Institute he was in charge of was the only thing that brought in important people from Madrid and Barcelona. The rest of it was a cultural wasteland. I said I agreed with him, but only to a point.

"Well, there's the Sala de Arte," I said. "Helena Román is doing important work there."

"It's true," noted Sonia, "just this week I saw an impressive video art exhibit there."

As soon as he heard this, Navarro jumped up off his stool as if something had stung him.

"Well, it's best if we don't say anything at all about Helena and her gallery space, since we're all here having a pleasant conversation."

I'd put my foot in it once again. Everybody knew that the relationship between Helena and Navarro was complicated. Even though their centers both belonged to the Community, there was a rivalry between them that was hard to understand. It seems that it all stemmed from the distant past. Navarro had been Helena's professor, and it annoyed him to see her triumph before he did. Although I was convinced that there was something more to it.

"The Sala de Arte is a reactionary place," he said, irritated. "They only show spineless, boring artists there."

I couldn't take it anymore.

"Well I wouldn't exactly say that Jacobo Montes is a spineless artist. I think I've heard enough."

"And who here said anything about Jacobo Montes?" asked Navarro.

"Montes is going to put on an exhibition at the Sala," I replied.

"Okay, man, there's no way that even Helena believes that's going to happen."

"I can prove it to you. I'm going to be his assistant while he prepares his piece here," I said with a bit of arrogance. And as soon as it came out, I regretted it. I don't know why I'd told someone like Navarro about that when I didn't even want to say anything to Sonia. It wasn't a secret—Helena had mentioned it to the whole class—but even so I was keeping it to myself. Nevertheless, I couldn't hold it in. Perhaps a need for notoriety and a certain sense of pride arose in me at that moment. Navarro hadn't stopped talking about all his travels and collaborations, and the critic, the few times that he'd opened his mouth, had made it perfectly clear that he thought he knew much more than the rest of us put together. Maybe that's why I mentioned the thing about Montes, to show them that I, too, could hold my own in that conversation.

"Hey," exclaimed Sonia, giving me a slap on the arm, "why didn't you say anything . . ."

"Well," interrupted Navarro, "if you say so, I guess I have to believe you. But that seems a little above Helena's pay grade. Or maybe"—he said, doubting himself for a moment—"it's not so absurd a possibility after all. Little Helena"—he said, emphasizing the pronunciation of each syllable—"worked with that lunatic a while back."

"Oh yeah?" I asked, surprised.

"She never told you about it?"

I shook my head.

"Ah, if you knew who Helena really was . . . A silly chick. But don't get me started on this, 'cause I'll go on for hours."

At that moment, the expression of boredom on the critic's face vanished, and he motioned with his head in a strange manner, as if he were repeatedly agreeing with what Navarro had just said, although he was looking off somewhere else. I followed his gaze and realized that it was directed at a young black man leaning against the wall. A few seconds later, the young man started to climb the stairs that led to the private rooms on the second floor.

"If you all will excuse me," said the critic, "I have to go up to the restroom for a moment."

I got the impression that he had new plans for the night. And I was happy for him. But I couldn't quite understand what happened next. As he passed by me, the critic put his hand on my shoulder and whispered in my ear something that left me stunned:

"Look, I don't know what this Helena character is like, but watch out for Montes. Maybe I shouldn't be telling you this, but that guy . . . he's the biggest son of a bitch on the face of the earth."

By the time I'd processed what he'd said and wanted to ask what he meant by it, the critic was already going up the staircase. Before disappearing behind the curtain, he looked back at me and put his index finger up to his temple, as if it were a pistol or, rather, as if he were telling me: "Don't forget. Remember my words. Don't say I didn't warn you."

I assumed that he wasn't going to come back downstairs for what remained of the night. And for a few moments I continued thinking about what he'd told me.

As soon as the critic disappeared, Navarro stopped talking about art and began to flirt with Sonia. His audience was gone and he no longer needed to impress anyone. Now he could concentrate on the only thing that really interested him.

Without taking his eyes off Sonia's cleavage, he asked us if we were a couple and if we lived together. Before we could reply, he told us that we were the best students he'd ever had and that we could count on him if we ever needed anything. Suddenly, he changed his posture on the stool, moistened his lips, and started staring intently at Sonia:

"You have to come by my office someday. I'll prepare the fountain of knowledge for you. If you drink from it, you'll be eternally wise and young."

"Wait, what . . ." she stammered out in surprise.

"It's a joke, woman. At this hour the kids are all in bed already and nothing's off limits."

Sonia shot me a conspiratorial look of disbelief at what she'd just heard. Navarro noticed it and told me:

"Don't think I'm jealous of you. If I were as close to this precious thing as you are and, as I'm guessing is your case, she'd never let me lay a finger on her, there'd be smoke billowing from my cock from jacking it so much."

At this point we were speechless. Navarro let out a loud laugh and slapped me on the back.

"Look, don't pay me any mind, I'm not feeling so hot. I'm sure it was something I ate at dinner," he said, still laughing. Then he took a sip of whatever he was drinking and continued: "All right, let's stop messing around here and go upstairs, all three of us. I'm treating you to something nice"—he said while sliding his hand into his pocket—"I got this from my Colombian guy."

Sonia was at a total loss for words. And it was all starting to make me cringe as well. Navarro had never been so explicit with us. At the end of the day, he was a public figure, and we were still just university students. I told him thanks, so as not to offend him, but that it would have to be some other time.

I gestured to Sonia, and she immediately understood. It was clear that the time had come for us to split.

"All right, whatever you want . . . And really, that stuff I said before was just a joke. I hope you aren't taking me seriously at this time of night and in this state."

And, after giving both of us a kiss on the cheeks, lingering somewhat over Sonia's face, he went upstairs, stumbling a little, then disappeared behind the curtains.

When we got out on the street, I felt the humid heat on my face. It wasn't even June yet, but the sweltering nights to come were already making themselves known. I walked Sonia to her building, and then quickly made my way back home. I don't remember having anything to drink, but I was extremely dizzy. My stomach and head hurt like I'd been drinking for days on end.

6

I slept terribly and woke up with an unbearable headache. "Montes is the biggest son of a bitch on the face of the earth." I heard the phrase repeatedly, like a mantra, while I lay awake before falling asleep and I woke up with the words on my lips, as if I'd been repeating them over and over in my sleep.

Montes was arriving on Monday. And even though I should have started studying and working on some papers for school, I decided to shut myself in my room for the weekend to learn as much as possible about him. I wanted to familiarize myself with his work, his references, his vocabulary. Even though, at the end of the day, I was merely taking him around from place to place in my car, I wanted to know everything. To impress him. Not to go unnoticed. Of course, he had met thousands of people and visited hundreds of places. I wasn't going to be the first student that assisted him. For that reason I wanted to get up to speed. And, to me, that meant knowing his work down to the last detail, knowing his origins, his ideas, his trajectory, his projects . . . so that I could have some amount of self-assurance when it came time to face him. At very least, I didn't want to disappoint Helena in any manner. I needed to demonstrate to her that she could trust me, that she'd made the right choice, that there was no one else in that city more prepared than I was to accompany Montes.

As such, I spent the weekend reading all the documents that I'd copied and pasted, looking at each and every one of the images I'd found on the internet, trying to absorb or organize everything that appeared on my computer screen. And I wasn't quite sure whether it all scared me or fascinated me.

I found some of the pieces beautiful and emotional, like the one in which he fulfilled the wishes of inmates in a Bolivian prison (*Liberty: A User's Manual*, 1996), or the series of hugs that he'd given to famous prisoners like Nelson Mandela and Antonio Negri (*Hugs are no longer useful, but they make our tears less wet*, 1990-1994). Other works were visually much more difficult for me, like the one carried out in 1992 on the discovery of America (*Slack Rope/Taking of Land*). In this piece, Montes—completely naked—walked along a slack rope emulating the feat of Philippe Petit between the Twin Towers. And, instead of keeping his balance, every so often he would speed up, jump slightly into the air, and land against the rope with his legs apart, the rope striking him in the testicles and anus. The piece ended when, after a large number of jumps, he had loosened the rope to such an extent that it touched the ground.

But, without a doubt, the pieces that made the biggest impact on me were those from the last few years, those from the period in which Montes had started to work with immigrants, using them to make invisible situations visible. Such was the case with his most widely known work at the time, *Bio-Paper*, carried out for the 2001 Lyon Biennale. In this piece, through lawyers and contacts at various embassies, Montes had obtained legal immigration papers for a number of undocumented Algerian immigrants, on the condition that they would allow the number of the resident card to be tattooed on their arm. A tattooed number—together with the wordplay that contained the term "Muslim"— which had been utilized in the concentration camps, and the idea of submission, connected the work to Giorgio Agamben's ideas about the state of exception and concentration camps as the biopolitical paradigm of the West.

This work had garnered him the praise of critics worldwide, who, from that moment on, began to celebrate him as the model of a socially engaged artist. Historians and critics like Benjamin Buchloh and Claire Bishop, and thinkers like Jacques Rancière and even Giorgio Agamben himself, had written various pieces about Montes that placed him at the summit of contemporary political art, far beyond the relational aesthetics and social art "light" of the nineties.

After reading all of this, it became even clearer to me that Montes was the central artist of the present and that no one had known as well as he did how to get to the heart of what was happening in the contemporary world. What I still hadn't been able to come to terms with completely was the bad taste left in the mouth after reckoning with his work. And not only because of the rawness of the images and performances, but rather, above all, because of the ultimate meaning behind them. An absolutely pessimistic and disillusioned vision of the world, which I was unsure if I wholly shared with him.

For Montes, there was no possible redemption. His theory of reproduction, about which he spoke in various interviews, left no room for doubt: we will never solve anything; only reproduce it. The artist, like everyone else, can only reproduce the logic of the system in which he finds himself stuck. For that reason, he never tried to prove anything, merely to show something that could not be changed. He simply showed. But he did it by reproducing reality, succumbing to the evil that he made visible. An evil that he could never denounce. Because the artist, for Montes, wasn't outside the world, but right in the middle of everything. The artist was guilty. His work stained the world. "Art is a dirty thing, and there is no way to clean it without it losing its color."

7

I arrived late to pick up Montes at the hotel. A taxi had brought him there from the airport, and he'd been in his room for over half an hour. I asked the receptionist to let him know I had arrived and that I was waiting in the lobby, ready to take him to the gallery.

The great artist was, in a few moments, going to come down to the lobby, and I couldn't calm my nerves. I felt as if I knew everything about him. I had read almost everything there was on the internet and in books. I couldn't have been more informed about his work and ideas. But, at the same time, I felt like I knew nothing about his real life. If he was friendly, if he had a sense of humor, if he was engaged to be married or had a partner, if he was attracted to men or women . . . I knew Montes the artist perfectly, but I was completely in the dark about Montes the person.

I would probably recognize him from the photos I'd seen, although I didn't have access to very many of them. Even though he was a famous, well-known artist, I'd barely found any pictures of him outside of the performances and actions. And, in the few that I'd seen, it always seemed like something was missing, as if it were impossible to capture his presence, or as if there were something about his presence that the image couldn't transmit entirely. Which was something I soon noticed when the elevator doors started to open. The distress was immediate. Time slowed down, and it took centuries for the doors to reveal the person inside. And there, surrounded by the multiplication of his own person in the mirrors, at long last, Montes appeared.

He was taller than I had imagined. And much slimmer. He was wearing a black shirt that went down to his knees and baggy pants that narrowed at the ankle. His shoes had an opening between the big toe and the other toes. He looked like a yoga master or a monk from some Eastern religion. But what caught my attention most was, without a doubt, the rotundity of his shaved head. A perfectly oval-shaped skull that would make one think of Brancusi except for the fact that the whiteness of the marble had there been replaced by a cluster of tattoos that barely left any scalp visible at all.

I had seen those tattoos in many photos of his performances, but here in person I was finally able to comprehend their true intensity. I immediately thought that, in all probability, he still had all the other adornments I'd seen on the rest of his body. The serpent that ran down his spine, or the Suprematist lines that he had had tattooed on his body in homage to Kasimir Malevich. For Montes—and this was one of the things that I'd read over the weekend—the body was a unique artistic surface. His skin was his greatest canvas. His canvas and the principal material of his work. Because he had not only just painted and decorated it; he had also stabbed it, burned it, scarred it, and slashed it.

His body, I thought, was a battlefield. And for a few seconds I was unsure whether or not I wanted to take part in that fight. I felt afraid, and it even crossed my mind to get out of there. He didn't know me. He wouldn't notice. And, further, deep down I only wanted to see him, to know that he really existed. And there I had him. The great artist whose work had fascinated me. Maybe I didn't need anything else. Or maybe I did. Of course I did. I needed more. Much more. I wanted to know everything. And that's why I was there. And so, after my brief hesitation, I got up out of my chair and went over to him.

"Señor Montes," I said. "I'm Marcos Torres. Helena Román sent me to take you to the gallery."

Montes stood there looking at me for a few seconds, as if my words had pulled him out of some inner world far from the present. Three small scars on his left cheek caught my attention. They were probably the result of *The Weight of Tears*, one of his most poetic performances. I had read about this piece, too. In the late 80s, Montes tattooed three small tears on his cheek. Then, with a scalpel, he tore them out, skin and all, and placed them in a tiny reliquary, emulating the lacrimal bottles from the Roman era, in which the remnants of the emotions of the great emperors were collected. The traces of those tears were no longer easily visible on his face, but they were still there, a small wound, a scar that made his face stand out and conferred a troubling aspect upon his gaze.

"Pleasure to meet you," he finally said, extending his right hand towards me. "Helena told me you'd be here. I hope you haven't been waiting too long."

His tone of voice—serious yet warm—and his words—gentle and perfectly pronounced, as if he were the presenter of a late-night radio call-in show, made me forget, for a moment, the dread that was coursing through my body. And even so, I couldn't help but know what I knew and remember what I had seen those last few days. The man I had right in front of me had done things that very few would be willing to do. And this was something I shouldn't have forgotten.

The mere fifteen minutes that separated the hotel from the Sala de Arte were sufficient for me to realize that Montes was nothing like anyone I had ever met up to that point. His presence nullified everything else.

All the way there, he asked questions nonstop about every little thing.

"What are the inhabitants of this city like? Are people happy here? Can you hear birds at night? How many suicides are there per year? Do artists gather at the park on Sundays? Do children look up at the sky when it's raining?"

It was like a machine gun. He linked together a series of questions one after the other, without any apparent commonality between them, and then he would suddenly go quiet and just observe the world around him.

I tried to respond to his questions, although I soon sensed that he wasn't really expecting answers. He didn't

70

seem to hear anything. It was as if his interrogatives were more like the externalization of thought than an attempt to establish a dialogue with me. More than asking questions, he seemed to be reciting verses.

He never stopped looking around and he seemed to take in every detail, as if he'd been let loose in a foreign country, as if nothing he observed were comprehensible to him. I noticed how he wrinkled up his brow and concentrated as he contemplated the trash cans or the plazas, as he looked at every last person, every last shop, every last window display we passed. He paused at every step he took. His rhythm was different from everyone else's. More than walking, he looked like he was floating through the air. Through a sluggish, heavy air.

At times I was fascinated and at others I was exasperated. And I recalled an image that I'd always found odd, that of the *flâneurs* walking with turtles on leashes down the narrow streets of old Paris. A slow, unhurried rhythm, a way of walking that was offbeat and against the flow, an extreme slowness that, in the midst of the twenty-first century, came off as disconcerting and disturbing.

One of the times that he stopped to look at a shop window, he fixed his gaze on the reflection of my face in the glass. And, without moving his eyes from my reflection, he said:

"So, you're going to be my assistant . . . I just hope you're not an aspiring artist."

He caught me off guard, and I didn't know how to respond. I just shook my head and ended up saying that no, I didn't want to be an artist, even though I was studying visual arts, and despite the fact that I was supposed to be preparing myself to become one. I told him that I liked thinking and reading more than creating images. And that just maybe, someday, I would even go on to write a doctoral dissertation, but that I'd never imagined exhibiting work in a gallery.

"That's good. There are already too many artists," he said, without taking his eyes off the glass window.

A second later, turning to look me in the face, he declared:

"I hope that we all die soon and stop sullying the world."

At that point, indeed, I was at a loss for words and preferred to keep quiet. And I don't think that he was waiting for my response. In fact, a few seconds later, he started up his slow stroll once more, without saying another word.

In a few short minutes we'd reached the city's main thoroughfare. For a moment, the street, with its bustle of cars and pedestrians, seemed monstrous and gigantic, and reminded me of the metropolises of science fiction films.

During the time that I had been walking with Montes, I had become infected by his rhythmic gait and his manner of looking at the world. And as I hurried through the crosswalk, I realized that, during the entirety of our short trip, Montes had literally taken me outside of time. As I crossed the main thoroughfare, however, the twitching, rapid rhythm of the city once again took over. But Montes kept walking at his slow pace. A few cars honked at him, but he was unperturbed. Aware that I'd returned to the present, I crossed at a quick clip. He, in turn, seemed to have no intention of changing his pace.

I looked at him from the sidewalk. And for an instant I thought I could see an invisible turtle at his side.

8

Helena gave Montes a hug and thanked me for bringing him there.

"This is my gallery. Well . . . your gallery," she said as she took him by the arm and led him inside.

I entered after them and followed them with my eyes.

The gallery was dimly lit. A series of projections filled the walls. It wasn't the first time I'd been in there. In fact, the Sala was the only space in the city that showed any contemporary art at all. But I still hadn't seen the exhibition that was on display at the time. *The Masks of Narcissus: Video Art and Self-Representation*, I read on one of the gallery walls.

"This exhibition," I could hear Helena explaining to Montes, "starts with Rosalind Krauss's arguments about video and the aesthetics of narcissism, then, little by little, shows that contemporary video artists have distanced themselves from the subjectivity and intimacy of the early days of video in order to attain a supposed, nearly neutral objectivity through the use of the mask as object."

"Video as a theatrical staging of a game of hide-and-seek," declared Montes.

"Yes, something like that. As always, you have the ability to put it into words better than anyone else."

Montes smiled. And continued to walk around the room, focusing his attention on the videos. Helena explained a few of the pieces to him, and Montes seemed to listen attentively to her. I stayed a few steps behind them at all times. But I could tell that there was a special complicity between the two of them. A relationship of mutual admiration and respect which made me think that, somewhere behind it all, there was a shared history. They were so natural and in tune with each other, something that doesn't happen in a professional relationship. Or at least that's what I thought.

When they reached the end of the exhibit, Helena turned to Montes:

"All right, is anything coming to you? Do you have a piece in mind? Video, performance, action . . . the gallery is yours and you can choose whatever you like. As long as you don't burn it down, of course, because the government minister would wring my neck."

"Nothing right now. I read a little about the city, very little, before coming here. And I'm certain that it's a good place to continue my research into the politics of immigration. But I want to do a specific piece about this place. I need some time to get familiar with the surroundings. I need some data to work with. And, above all, I need some experiences . . ."

"It's the only thing worth a damn," interrupted Helena, uttering this phrase at the same time as Montes. "I remember."

They looked at each other again as if this phrase were some sort of secret password. I felt like I was completely outside of the synchrony they had between the two of them.

"If you want," Helena said after a few seconds, "we can go into my office and discuss some of the thornier issues. Budget, dates, technical matters . . ."

Montes agreed. And then Helena turned to me:

"You don't mind waiting here for a few minutes, right?" I shook my head. "Tell the security guard to give you a catalogue and take a look at it. I don't think we'll be more than fifteen minutes. But don't leave. We'll need you afterwards to take Jacobo to the hotel."

For a moment, I felt like I'd been kicked out. The two of them had some sort of shared world in which I didn't seem to fit. But what was I expecting? Further, I'd already had enough. I'd met Montes. I couldn't ask for more. So I remained there, waiting, wandering around the darkened gallery, among the images and sounds of the videos on the screens.

I became completely engrossed in one of the pieces in the exhibition. In the video, a man appeared—wearing a dark suit and a white shirt, his head shaved, and a mirrored mask covering his face—walking at night through a city that looked to be in Central Europe and which I soon found out was Prague. The echo of his footsteps in the empty streets and the sound of breathing from behind the mask conferred a hypnotic character upon the images.

The man in the mask's gait immediately reminded me of Montes. On the way from the hotel to the Sala de Arte, I had noticed that he looked at the world as if everything were strange, as if everything were reflected in his mask. And I thought that, in some way, for a few moments, I, too, had put on this mirrored mask, that everything had seemed new to me, and that I had distanced myself from everything that was right before my eyes, transforming, fleetingly, into an object.

The end of the video showed the walking man looking at what appeared to be the rosette of a cathedral. The man remained there for a few seconds. The rosette on the façade of the building was thus reflected in the mask, and the reflection seemed to transform into a giant eye. It was as if one didn't know who was doing the looking—the man or the building itself—and the distance between being an object and being a subject dissolved completely. As if everything there had vanished for good. An eye, that of the rosette, which looked like an abyss, a black hole, a drain down which everything might escape. And the mask seemed to me, at that moment, like a way of protecting oneself against that dark emptiness that calls out to us time and again. I felt a trembling in my body and a sense of dread unknown to me. I recalled the conversation with Montes in front of the glass of the shop window, and I imagined his eyes looking at me as if they were an abyss. And his words struck me again. Soon we will all be dead and we will no longer sully the world.

"It's beautiful, right?"

Helena's voice brought me out of a state that seemed a lot like meditation. I don't know how long I had been there watching the video, hypnotized by the echo of the footsteps and the sound of breathing, bewitched by that melodious rhythm, sitting in a corner of the gallery, wrapped up in the images, protected by the darkness.

Helena appeared amid the shadows like a phantom. I stood up and walked outside the gallery with her. The light of the real world left me momentarily blinded. When I opened my eyes, I could see the backlit image of Montes.

"Jacobo would like to visit some places around town this afternoon," said Helena. "He wants to see the neighborhoods on the outskirts and start to get an idea of what the situation is like there."

"Not a problem at all," I said.

"The outside is the shape of the inside," declared Montes, as if he were poetically arguing his reasons for needing to see those places.

Helena then told me that I could pick him up at the hotel around five in the afternoon. For now, there was no need for me to accompany him. She wasn't going to be available in the afternoon, so they were going to get lunch together and continue sorting out some issues regarding the exhibition. But it was certainly going to be a productive workday. Montes needed this initial contact. And then I'd take him back to the hotel.

Helena gave me all of these instructions, and Montes distractedly looked on, as if it all had nothing to do with him. When she finished telling me all this and they both went back into the gallery, I decided to head straight home to eat something. While I was making myself a cheese sandwich in the kitchen, I felt that I had returned to reality. But I also noticed that this reality wasn't the same one from the day before. In some way, Montes had traveled through it. I intuited that something had begun to change.

9

"You always have to start with the places of transit. They're the doors that connect two worlds. At the threshold is the origin of all things. They're like magnetic poles that never quite let us leave entirely."

This is what Montes said when we arrived at the bus station. They were practically the first words he'd spoken since I picked him up at the hotel. Few words that nevertheless, made me think. It had never occurred to me. But he had a point. The two main immigrant neighborhoods in the city were centered around the train station and the bus station, as if living there made the immigrants, at least symbolically, closer to home.

At the bus station, I focused my attention on the movement of suitcases, on the constant departure of buses, and on the transfer of people from one place to another. There was much more movement than I could ever have imagined. And, at the same time, it was repetitive movement. The same gestures, the same routines. Everyone was, at once, both the same and different.

At the train station I observed similar scenes. And again the amount of people sitting on benches caught my attention. They weren't all traveling. Many of them didn't have a suitcase. They were just there: seated, motionless, as if they were waiting for something that never seemed to arrive completely, as if the waiting had taken hold of them.

Montes remained silent the entire time. He just watched. He observed everything attentively and occasionally jotted something down in a black notebook that he kept in one of his pockets. He didn't talk to anybody, didn't ask any questions, nor did he take any photos of the things he saw. That puzzled me. Instead of someone documenting experiences for his work, he seemed more like a tourist who'd decided to go out for a stroll.

When night began to fall, we sat down on a bench in a park on the outskirts of town. And only then did Montes start talking again.

"Ultimately, it's about knowing how to look."

"What?" I asked.

"Art," he said. And, after a short pause, he continued: "It's a form of knowing how to look. That's the only thing that matters. The rest is excess. The rest is nothing more than the rest. What we do afterwards is a manner of telling others what we have seen. But the important thing is what we have seen, not what we're going to say. Art is a way of telling. But above all it's a way of looking."

I nodded in agreement and stayed quiet. Montes was talking about art. It was moving to listen to his words. This was the moment I had hoped for. He was telling me what art was to him. To the great artist. And he was saying all this to me, a nobody, in the middle of that dark park, in that tiny town, completely off the radar of art history.

"Each work is a frustrated conclusion. The result is the least important part. What matters is the experience. The process, thinking, doing, feeling, seeing . . . all of that is the work of art. And at the end a mere trace remains. And that is what people see. But that's what matters the least. The only important thing is what you've seen, what you've felt, what you've experienced."

He then turned towards me and, for the first time, said my name.

"Marcos, I want to know everything. I want to feel everything. And for the next month I need you to be my eyes here. My eyes, my hands, and my emotions. And I need a commitment on your part."

"Of course," I replied.

"I want you to understand that this is art."

I agreed without question.

"I'll only tell you one more thing: what we're going to do here is very important. It's not a work. It's life. We are playing with life. Our lives and those of others. Art is a game of life and death. If you don't understand it that way, it's all just a disgusting lie."

"You can count on me for anything you need," I said without thinking. "I promise to risk my life for it."

An instant later I realized to whom I had spoken those words. I had just made a promise to Jacobo Montes. I was well aware of how far things could go. A chill ran over my entire body. Even so, I trusted that his use of those words hadn't been literal.

Montes then explained to me what my work was going to consist of. We had dedicated an entire afternoon to seeing and feeling. That was the first step. And I was going to have to be in charge of the second. He would return in a month and start working on the materials I would gather in the interim. I would have to send him information, collect experiences, do everything that he told me to do. We would communicate by e-mail and, if necessary, by telephone. And I would have a small desk for the paperwork I was going to need to do in the Sala de Arte, next to Helena's office.

I wasn't exactly sure why, but it seemed like Montes trusted me completely. Perhaps much more than I was even able to trust myself.

I took him back to the hotel. His plane was leaving early the next day, and he didn't want to go to sleep too late. He still had to finish up some things before he continued his trip. Our town had just been one stop. Other places around the globe were also awaiting his work.

He would contact me soon and give me further instructions. For now, the only thing I had to do was look. Discover what was all around me. Contemplate the world as if it were the last time I was passing through it.

"When everything disappears forever," he said as he got in the elevator, "all that we'll have left is a mere trace in our pupils."

A few seconds later—at that point, time had truly sped up—the doors closed, and Montes disappeared entirely. In truth, traces of his images remained in my retina for a few moments. A fleeting impression that, nonetheless, I knew for certain I would never be able to erase.

II. THE INVISIBLE CITY

1

It wasn't entirely clear to me what it meant to be an artist's assistant. Nor did I even know if I was really Montes's assistant. I only knew that I had to be his eyes in the city. And that's what I tried to do. So for a few days I devoted myself to going on walks, looking, observing the world the way Montes had told me to. I sat in parks, looked, took note of routines, of comings and goings, listened in on conversations, paid attention to everything going on around me. I tried to observe the world as if it were the last time I was passing through it.

Less than two days later, I received an e-mail from Montes. He had started thinking about something. Something important, he said. But he was going to need some data before he began to develop his work. He wanted me to send him, as soon as possible, some information about immigration in the city. Real facts. Nothing official. Data that wasn't contaminated. Data born of experience. "Data of resistance," he wrote. I didn't quite know what that was, even though I more or less intuited what he meant.

That was when I thought about turning to some association or NGO that assisted immigrants. I didn't know very much about it. There had to be a few dozen of them. So I was unsure where to start.

Just a few minutes later I had the answer. Sonia. I seemed to recall that she had a friend who worked on that sort of thing, although I couldn't remember very well.

"Yes, her name is Ana Ruiz," she told me when I gave her a call. "She's a volunteer at"—she hesitated for a moment—"City Refuge, although I'm not totally sure about that. Write down the number."

While I wrote it down, I heard moaning on her end of the phone.

"Sorry, Marcos, it's my dad . . . I have to let you go."

"Is everything all right?" I asked.

"Just fine. Don't worry about it. You've got other things to worry about. Tell Ana that I say hello, I haven't seen her in ages, and let's get together some afternoon so that you can catch me up on that mysterious man."

I said goodbye to her, knowing that everything wasn't just fine, and as soon as I hung up, I called Ana. Her voice sounded pleasant to me. Of course, she said, she'd be happy to help me with whatever I needed. I could swing by the office whenever I wanted. The organization really was called City Refuge and was close to the bus station and across the street from the health clinic, right in the center of one of the immigrant neighborhoods.

That same morning I went to the address she had given me. The office was small and looked more like a room of a house. Two desks with computers, three file cabinets, and little else. And all of it was dominated by an enormous cork bulletin board covered in layers of announcements printed on colored paper.

"Hi . . . Ana Ruiz?" I asked rhetorically. She was the only one there.

"Here, present," she said, raising her hand as if she were in grade school. "You must be Sonia's friend."

"Marcos."

"That's right. I've got a terrible head for names, but I remember faces."

Her face, however, wasn't familiar to me at all. Light-colored eyes, black hair that was buzzed close to the scalp, a piercing in the middle of her lower lip. She looked like a guy. An ambiguous, attractive guy. It obviously wasn't a face that was easy to forget.

"Have a seat," she said, indicating one of the chairs in front of her desk. "How's Sonia? I haven't seen her since before Christmas."

"Well, she's still . . ."

"What shit luck, that stuff with her dad. Hopefully that all gets resolved. But that's life. My god, if I were to tell you . . . But why don't you tell me something, that's why you've come here."

I then told her that I needed information about immigration in the city.

"Oh, that's it? Information?" she said ironically.

I nodded affirmatively, a little embarrassed at the naivety of my request.

"Well, man . . . there's a lot, all that you could want. Look." She pointed at one of the file cabinets. "That's full of documents. Each person that comes to us for help is a distinct case. And you wouldn't believe what there is out there."

"Perhaps I need something more general," I clarified. "I don't know, something to give me an initial idea of the situation."

"Initial idea? I can give you that: it's shitty. The shittiest."

"I bet, but . . ."

"I know, I get it . . ." she interrupted. "There's a series of preliminary studies, surveys, and reports that will help you get your . . . initial idea," she said, emphasizing my words.

"That would be perfect. Is it possible to access them?"

"I can give you all of it, right now," she replied resolutely. "If you can wait a few minutes, I'll burn you a CD with all the information. And if you want, I can also give you the contact information of some of the members of the association who have worked on these reports."

"Fantastic."

"Strength in unity," she added.

While she was burning the CD, Ana asked me about my work. I told her that I was studying visual arts and that I needed the information for an artist who was going to do a piece on immigration in the city. She was surprised. She couldn't imagine why an artist would be mixed up in all that. I explained to her that artists these days didn't just paint or sculpt, that many of them worked as if they were sociologists or anthropologists, and that some, like Montes, did pieces that attempted to call attention to invisible or unjust situations.

"Well, you're going to find a ton of those in all this stuff," she said, while she stood up to put away some files.

At this point, I was able to see her body for the first time. I focused on her tiny, thin legs, which looked like they were straight out of a children's cartoon.

"Right before you got here," she explained, "there was a Moroccan woman here who is going to have to have a breast removed. She's been diagnosed with cancer and they're giving her chemotherapy. But she has to keep taking care of the elderly woman she works for. She's undocumented and doesn't know what to do. Her family is in Morocco. But she can't travel because she's sick. Nor can any of her family come visit her. And she can't stop working because she needs the money. Unjust? Invisible?"

I just stared at her, not knowing what to say.

"We've sent an e-mail out to our volunteers. Someone has to take care of her. And this isn't the first case like this. Immigrants also get sick, you know?"

"Yeah. I suppose so."

"Sometimes we think about them like their only problem is finding work so they can send money home. Or get legal documents. But it's much more complex than that. Invisible situations, as you say. Tell your artist to focus on that. Have you ever seen anything more unjust? That poor woman goes into the phone booth and talks to her family and tells them that everything is fine, so they don't worry."

"And what about the elderly woman's family? Wouldn't they have the decency to let her go on leave if they found out she was sick?"

"Would they? What would you do? People aren't NGOs. They'll end up firing her. They aren't going to pay someone to take care of both the elderly woman and the caretaker. It's understandable, artist. That's the worst part, that it's understandable."

"Well I wouldn't . . ."

"We never know how we are going to act in certain situations until we're right in the middle of them."

"But there are norms of humane behavior that one always knows of a certainty they would never . . ." I was unsure how to continue this line of argumentation. "I don't know, a human life is a human life. And that is above all else."

"You're an idealist, are you? So am I. That's why I'm here. Although with this job, I've got to get back on the horse after falling off day after day."

She then looked firmly at me and said:

"Maybe you should spend some time here. Your help would be welcome. And it would certainly be useful for your research and for your artist."

"But what could I do?"

"A lot. You know how to read and write. So you could already teach classes. You wouldn't imagine how much you could help us out."

"I'll think about it," I said.

"Don't think too much about it. These are the kinds of things that, if you think too much about them, you'll always end up finding the perfect excuse not to do them."

"No, no, I'm sure I'll find some time to be able to do something."

"I'll take your word for it . . . artist."

Ana gave me the CD. I thanked her for her kindness and said goodbye, telling her that when my exams were over and I'd finished the research for Montes, I'd lend a hand with anything they needed.

"Don't doubt it," I asserted.

Deep down, I knew I was lying.

2

After leaving the office, I decided to head over to the Sala de Arte. I was excited to see the space that Helena had set aside for me. And I wanted to send Montes the information I'd gathered as soon as possible, so he could start outlining his work.

The Sala wasn't too far from there, just a few streets over towards the center of town. The quickest route was straight through the immigrant neighborhood. Plus, going that way, I'd be able to slide back into my role as occasional anthropologist.

While I walked through those streets, I observed everything anew. Butcher shops, hair salons, clothing shops, small cafés . . . it all provided an image of a completely different city. And for a few moments I felt like I was far, far away. I imagined that the residents of the neighborhood must also have felt something similar, but inverted. Walking through these streets was perhaps, to them, a way of feeling at home. And it suddenly seemed like close and far were dimensions that lost all meaning here. Or perhaps that was only my perception of it. Perhaps it wasn't such a simple thing, and a street was still just a street, far was still far, and this strange world was, at bottom, nothing more than a neighborhood in my city.

In less than five minutes I was back in the real city. As I passed by the supermarket that was near the Sala de Arte, the distance faded away and the city returned to its rightful place. However, seconds later, as I looked around, everything seemed strange to me again. There was nothing there that was closer or further away from what I'd just seen in the immigrant neighborhood. The parked cars, the photo shop, the packages of tobacco at the tobacco shop, the parking meter in the blue parking zone, the advertisement for perfume on the awning of the bus stop, the smell of kebab at the end of the street, the delivery van unloading goods at the convent across the street, the shoes of the passersby, their clothes, their voices, the looks on their faces, their gestures, their way of talking on their cell phones . . . the distances had faded away. I no longer knew for sure where it was that I believed I'd returned to and even doubted the existence of a place to return to at all. I then imagined that the immigrant neighborhood was a concentrated version of the entire city, that everything was now very far away, and that the "here," this place that told us who we were, had begun to disappear from the map. I realized that living in the city had transformed into a manner of being far away. And for the first time in a long while I felt absolutely lost. If, as I had walked through the immigrant neighborhood, I had felt distance, now, at home—in what I believed, supposed, thought, and presumed to be my home—I noticed that distance pervaded all things.

With this strange sensation, I entered the Sala de Arte almost as if I were seeking refuge. The darkness and the continual murmur of the videos in the exhibition wrapped themselves around me and, paradoxically, the ghostly images ended up bringing me back to reality.

Helena wasn't in, but she had left instructions for them to show me where my space would be. The security guard led me over to the offices. After opening the door in one of the corners of the gallery, he took me into the office space through a hallway full of unopened boxes and paintings stacked up against the wall.

"You can also come in straight from the street through the other door," he told me as we arrived at my spot.

The space wasn't excessively large, but sufficient enough that five or six people could work there comfortably. There was a sort of reception area with a sofa and a coffee table. The rest of the office was broken up into offices by glass walls covered with some vinyl decals of the Community logo.

The security guard showed me one of the offices. It was empty, and I could use it whenever I wanted. It wasn't going to be used by anyone for a few months.

"I'll be here if you need anything. Helena's office is this one," he said, pointing to the door right across the hall.

I thanked him and said goodbye.

I was surprised by what I found there. A wooden, L-shaped desk, a swivel-chair, computer, telephone, scanner, printer, bookshelves, a file cabinet that went up to the ceiling . . . I thought I was going to have a small nook set off in a corner somewhere, yet I had found an ideal place to work.

I quickly took possession of the space. I put the folders that Ana had given me on the desk and turned on the computer. The chair was comfortable, much more than the one I had in my bedroom. So it immediately occurred to me that I should study there during the exam period. And I also noticed that the temporary office that nobody used was larger, more modern, and better equipped than the one Ana had at City Refuge. I felt guilty for a moment. Perhaps for that reason I got to work without a minute's delay.

I leafed through the documents and examined the contents of the CD before sending it off to Montes. I opened each of the files one by one to make sure they worked. I found reports, statistics, graphics, photographs, and presentations. Files of all sorts, .doc, .xls, .jpg, .tiff, .ppt . . . enough material for weeks' worth of work. Everything seemed to be in order. So I sent the majority of the files over the course of a few e-mails. I decided to send the ones that were too large along with the printed documents to Montes's studio in New York via express mail. The Sala would take care of it all.

While the e-mail attachments were uploading, I printed out a few documents to get an initial idea—I smiled as I thought about this expression—of the situation.

Between 1993 and 2003, more than 50,000 immigrants had arrived in the Community. It was the province with the fifth most immigrants in the country. The percentage of immigrants was almost 5% of the population. The countries of origin were mainly Ecuador (39%), Morocco (31%), Colombia (5.76%), Ukraine (3.59%), and Bolivia, Algeria, and Sudan (2%). The rest of the percentages were under 2%. But you could say that there were immigrants from practically every country in the world.

According to the anthropologists' reports, there were three essential groups. Africans, Latin Americans, and Eastern Europeans. I was surprised that the Chinese didn't appear on any of the lists.

The majority of the reports centered on work. They were classified by gender and country of origin. Domestic work: women, chiefly Latin Americans; service sector: Latin Americans, men and women; farm work: Maghrebis, chiefly from Algeria and Morocco, men; construction: Sub-Saharans, men; other industries: Ukrainians, Bulgarians, and Lithuanians, men. The Chinese, once again, were left off.

It was all data. Percentages, numbers, pure abstraction. I couldn't get a grasp on what this all represented. But even so, I believed that this was already a start. And I waited for Montes to make his move.

It didn't take too long for the move to happen. That night, before going to bed, I received an e-mail from him. He thanked me for what I'd sent and told me that the data gave him more than enough for what he had started to conceive. He was sure that there was much more information at every level, but that with this, he had enough. The only thing that he was going to need, and which wasn't among the data that I'd sent him, was some information about the internet cafés in the city. His piece, he said, was probably going to revolve around problems of communication and the isolation of speaking a foreign language, an issue to which he had dedicated some of his recent work. As such, he asked me to send him, as soon as possible, a list of all the internet cafés in the city, with their addresses and the nationality of their owners. As well as a photo of each place. A shot of both the exterior and the interior. And the most important thing was that I send him everything through the internet café, as if I were just another customer. He was interested in the data, but, above all, the experience. I was to observe, analyze, feel. This is what differentiated art from sociology. "Data is always erroneous," he wrote, "though we can't escape it. But experiences are never wrong. Art is a form of experience."

As I read the last sentence of his e-mail, I once again felt privileged. A simple e-mail had been transformed into a theory of art. My Hotmail account had suddenly become a receptacle for the sort of statement that I once only read in books. I went to bed feeling like I was a part of something important.

3

The next morning, I called Ana and asked if the association had a list of internet cafés in the city. She remembered who I was, the artist, and told me that they had a sort of directory with the names and addresses of many of them. She could send it to me via e-mail in a few minutes.

Her e-mail didn't take long to arrive. Names, addresses, and contact persons. Twenty-five internet cafés in the whole city. My Land, My Children, The Andes, My Country, Here and There, The Home, Nostalgia, UniWorld . . . Judging by the names of the contact people, the majority of the establishments seemed to be run by Latin Americans, and only a few by Africans. None by Europeans or Asians.

I printed out the document, bought a map of the city, and marked with an X the location of each of the internet cafés. Then I traced a sort of route and numbered the establishments in the order I planned to visit them. I wanted to calculate how much time it would take to get from one to the next and how much time I would spend at each of them. For some reason I suspected that Montes would be interested in this sort of planning.

When I finished sketching out the route, I realized that what had appeared on the map was a sort of circle that only rarely moved towards the city center. Surprisingly, the line almost coincided with the outline of the ancient Arab city wall. It was curious, the outskirts were still the outskirts.

With this material, and armed with my camera, I spent practically the entire morning and part of the afternoon going in and out of the internet cafés, always with the same routine. I'd arrive, jot down the time, take a picture of the exterior, enter, briefly introduce myself, ask permission, take a picture of the interior, then jot down on the map the amount of time I'd spent there. I didn't want to be an artist, I was convinced of this, but I was also aware that what I was doing bore a certain family resemblance with action pieces of more than one artist I knew.

The internet café from which I sent all the information to Montes was called My Land. It was located on the route towards the bus station and its yellow façade could be seen from almost anywhere along the street. It called to mind Van Gogh's house at Arles, with its bold yellow and dark blue accents. There I scanned the brochures and sent an e-mail to Montes recounting my experience, attaching the directory that Ana had sent me as well. I also sent him a package with some CDs of the pictures I had taken over the course of the day and the map with my annotations.

Before sending it all to him, I asked the manager of the place a few questions in order to contextualize my experience. He was a young Latin American guy who couldn't have been more than thirty years old. He told me that he was Bolivian and that back in his country he had worked as a journalist, but that he was working there in the internet café until he could find something else.

"At the end of the day," I said, "it's also a form of communication."

When I asked him about his work in the internet café and the experiences he lived through every day, I was surprised by his articulate speech and his perfectly constructed discourse.

"The internet has contributed to bringing families together. The methods we have for getting accustomed to the realities of living abroad are curious. Here, we try to create a world of refuge, a place where anyone can feel close to their homeland. It's a sort of window into their homes. Back in Bolivia, internet cafés are places we're envious of. A lot of people dream about being able to go in. Because going in means that there's someone on the other side, or that you yourself intend on getting out and crossing the ocean." He barely moved while he spoke, as if he were giving a news report in front of an invisible camera. "The internet café is like the first step in leaving. Here, however, people look down on us, because only immigrants frequent these places. You all have internet and telephones at home. But most of us don't. Thus, it's like we're at home here. What's more, we try to make it so that aside from being a place of longing, this is also a place of happiness. We have a lot of products, music, and movies from back home. Sometimes it's hard to find blank cassettes so we can copy the tapes, but we always find a way."

I listened to the young man as if I were at a conference, without interrupting him at any point and trying to absorb everything that he said. He had a good point. I agreed with him completely. It was easy to see the purpose of a shop where you did things that you could do at home. Sending an e-mail, making a phone call, or printing out a picture were all things usually done in private. But at the internet café, the private and the public were mixed together. The individual and the collective overlapped.

When he finished his musings, I thanked him and asked if I could stick around for a while and watch how it all worked.

"Of course, we've got all the time in the world here," he said, gesturing towards some clocks on the wall that were decorated with the flags of Bolivia, Colombia, and Brazil, "take your pick."

It then occurred to me to call home and talk to my mom. It had been more than a week since I'd last called her. And it seemed like the ideal place to do it. That way I could experience what it was like inside one of the booths.

Before I could even get a word out, my mom scolded me about how long it had been since she'd heard anything from me.

"One day you're going to forget the phone number."

I told her that I'd been very busy finishing up papers and that I only had a minute to talk. I also told her that I'd started helping out an artist and that I was going to have to stay in town for a few more weeks until that was all over.

"We're getting older, son. And when you're not here, time passes faster and it seems like it's all just lost."

"I know, Mom, but . . ."

Deep down, I knew she was right. I barely ever thought of them. And I justified it by thinking that I'd soon have time to spend with them, that for now it was my time and I had to take advantage of it. Over the years, I've learned that no one ever has their own time, that there's no future in which you can put your trust in things, and that everything you don't do, like she had said, is just lost forever.

"At least call more often," she said sorrowfully as we said goodbye.

"I will, don't worry."

After I hung up, I stayed in the booth for a moment, preoccupied, shielded by that strange privacy. Talking on the phone in that place was like taking a leap into the past. It brought back memories of the time when my family didn't have a telephone in our home and my mom had to make calls from the lone bar in town. I was very little, but it was all still clear in my head. Above all else, I remembered how it felt like a rare treat when someone went out to make a call. "We're going to go call Uncle Emilio," my mom would say. And when she came back, my dad would ask her how they were doing. Making a phone call in those days was "going out to make a phone call," it implied a displacement. And sometimes I felt like, in effect, we were going out to and coming back from a place that was closer to Uncle Emilio's house than to our own.

Things were different now and everything had changed. That's what I thought at first. But then I realized that this change had not taken place completely, or at least not everywhere. I observed the goings on in the internet café closely and noticed that, there, people were still "going out to make a phone call," and that, for them, this place was still closer to home than other places were. Certain modes of experience still existed there that had disappeared in other places. It was as if things were moving at different speeds and hadn't disappeared entirely, as if everything overlapped with everything else and different worlds crossed paths with each other. I only had to look around me. At the internet café, all time periods had their place. Video chat coexisted with wire transfers of money, e-mail with postcards, printing of digital images with photographs that were dropped off to be developed, DVDs and CDs with cassette tapes and VHS videos. And it all functioned and continued to serve its original purpose. There was no place for obsolescence. Time there was multiple and complex.

I again glanced over at the clocks on the wall with their different time zones and thought that time here was not only the chronological time of day, but that there was much more implicit in that time. At bottom, everything was a matter of time. The time you wait, the time you work, the time of your experiences, the time of your life. To immigrate, I thought, was to move in space, to go from one place to another, but, even more than that, it was also to move in time. The immigrant is—and this became clear to me at that moment—a voyager who travels through time and who always

105

inhabits a time that is not his. And the thing was that among all the clocks hung up on the wall, there was one that offered a time that dominated the others: the clock with the Spanish flag, which kept the time that you had to align yourself with. That was the measurement of things. That was the time that reigned outside. Although there, among all the other clocks, it was just one more time. Perhaps, as the young man at the internet café had said, one could still take one's pick.

I spent my afternoon in these digressions. And little by little the internet café started to fill up with customers. Some made phone calls, others got more minutes on their cell phones, some sent e-mails, and a lot of them used the webcams to see their families.

I became captivated by a video chat between a young Latin American woman and a little girl. The young woman had on headphones with a microphone and she watched an image that hardly moved on the screen. She sat there watching the little girl for over five minutes, without saying a word.

"Her name is Dolores," the manager of the internet café whispered to me. "She comes in every Friday afternoon and talks to her little daughter. She's been here for a few years and the little one is with her grandmother back in Bolivia."

"But they don't say anything," I pointed out.

"It's the bandwidth back in El Alto. It's better to keep quiet to keep the image from freezing up. It's normal. Because of that, a lot of people talk on the phone first and then watch the images. But even so, it's still magical."

Mother and daughter watched each other almost without moving. One facing the other, as if they could feel the image beating, knowing that there was something behind it, a presence they could believe in at least a little bit. Those images were something more than a photograph and something less than a video. They stood midway between the fixed image and the moving image. I thought that some day an artist should work on that strange regime of images.

What was clear, in any case, was that time and space inside the internet café were different and that the rules and norms of everyday life didn't hold sway there. Perhaps it was, indeed, a magical place, although it was second-hand magic. But it was magic nonetheless. And I could see it in Dolores's eyes, even in the delayed image whose occasional movement was celebrated as if it were a gift. Without a doubt, that was a place of hope. A thin ray of light in the midst of the darkness.

Montes had a good eye for choosing a space for his material. After a few days, I received a message from him congratulating me on the research and telling me that he had started to develop the piece. He had conceived of an "intense and brutal" action—those were his words. He wasn't going to disclose anything to me at the moment. But he assured me that he had managed to combine anguish and hope in a single piece. I'd soon learn more details.

Even though he didn't need any more data at the moment, he asked me to keep collecting experiences and, above all, to search for something that was both tragic and unknown.

"I need extreme situations. There's still a lot to do. I'm certain that you'll find something where you least expect it. Something more. Search for human tragedy. The most obvious and the most invisible. That which no one wants to see. The worst things are always right under our noses. Remember the Poe story: the best way to hide something is to put it where everyone can see it."

4

Saturday night, as I arrived home after spending the afternoon in the library, I found Sonia sitting on the sofa in the living room.

"Your roommate let me in," she said in a hoarse voice. Then I noticed that her eyes were red.

"What's going on?"

"It's my dad . . . I can't take it any more." She let out a single sob.

"It's okay, calm down." I took her hands in mine. "You'll see, everything is going to work out okay."

"No, Marcos, it's not, it's getting worse. We went to the hospital again today and the doctor said that the possibilities are slim." She sat in silence for a moment, staring blankly, then said in anger: "Fuck. Why is this happening to him? He spent his whole shitty life working, and now that he has some free time . . ."

I bit at my lips, not knowing what to say.

"This is bullshit, Marcos, a huge pile of bullshit."

"It's okay, it's okay, you'll see . . ." I finally stammered out. And just as those words came out of my mouth, I started to feel ridiculous. How could I console her? I knew nothing of life. I was really young when my grandfather died. And I'd never had to endure an illness in the family.

"I'm sorry, Marcos, really. It's just that I don't know who else I can vent to. I don't want to act like this in front of my mom. She already has enough to deal with. And my dad still doesn't know a thing."

"I understand," I weakly whispered.

"I have to be strong in front of everyone else. And I try, you know? My dad says that I'm the source of joy in the house and if I could bottle that medicine, everyone would be cured. But sometimes I just can't take it. Today, when the doctor told us all this, I consoled my mom and acted like the strong one. And then at home, in front of my dad, acted like nothing had happened. 'Everything's great, Dad, you run on Duracell batteries and will end up outliving us all.' And inside, shit, in pieces."

I still wasn't sure, at all, what I should say and how I should say it. And I consoled myself by believing that it was best just to nod, look at her, touch her . . . just to be there. Sometimes one's mere presence is enough. That's what I thought as I gritted my teeth, searching fruitlessly for a word of encouragement.

Little by little, Sonia began to calm down. She just needed to talk, to say everything that she had to keep quiet at home. And I felt honored that she trusted me in that way.

"This is all such fucking shit," she concluded, this time huffing out of a sense of being fed up more than anything else. Then she adjusted her position on the sofa, turned to me, and said: "Marcos . . . you know something?"

"What?"

"I need to get high and get laid tonight."

I felt a little disoriented, trying to make sense of her words. And, after a few seconds, I was able to reply:

"I'm afraid I'm not the most ideal person for satisfying your desires."

She laughed for the first time. And then said:

"I know you're all tied up with your papers and the thing with Montes—which, by the way, I'm such an idiot, I haven't even asked you about—but if you could go out with me for a little bit tonight . . . Just for a tiny little while . . . then you can just leave me by myself, all right?"

She still looked like she'd been crying, but her face had begun to shine again. And I couldn't tell her no, even though I didn't like that sort of thing back then. So I ended up giving in.

I went into my bedroom for a moment to change clothes. One black shirt for another. At least the new one smelled good. I looked at myself in the mirror before leaving. I looked like I a seminarian out on a field trip. It wasn't unusual for priests to wave hello to me out on the street.

From the hallway, I could hear Sonia talking on her cell phone:

"We'll see you soon. I'm going to smoke every last thing in this town."

I gestured that I was ready to go and waited for her by the door. She picked up her purse and, right before she reached me, hung up her call and snapped her phone closed with the sound of a castanet.

"All set," she exclaimed.

"Professional, very professional," I said, imitating the Galician accent of Manuel Manquiña in the film *Airbag*.

Sonia laughed. And I would have loved to lose myself in her smile.

We arrived at Indie, one of the fashionable bars, in less than ten minutes. They had live music there on Saturdays, but there was still a spot for us at a corner of the bar.

"Here, hidden away," said Sonia, taking refuge behind a pillar covered in flyers for bands I didn't know.

She ordered a vodka with lime, and I ordered a Coca-Cola. And before we could make ourselves comfortable, someone put their hand on my back.

"The artist! We're seeing each other everywhere these days."

It was Ana, who immediately gave Sonia a hug and greeted her with two kisses to the cheeks.

"You're a lifesaver," said Sonia. And I instantly deduced whom it was she'd been talking to on her cell.

Ana grabbed a barstool and sat between us. At that moment, an intense smell of soap wafted over me. Her short hair was completely wet, as if she had just hopped out of the shower. When she lifted her arm to order a beer, I could tell that she wasn't wearing a bra and noticed the movement of her small breasts underneath her white tank top. I tried to avert my eyes, although I wasn't entirely successful.

While they were getting her beer, Ana took a bar of hash out of her purse, carefully unwrapped it, and offered it to Sonia. With deft movements, Sonia cut off a large piece, softened it with the flame of her lighter, crushed it between her fingers, and mixed it with a little tobacco. I was enchanted by the ritual.

"Easy there, lady," said Ana, "you've gotta be able to walk out of here on your own two feet."

"Gah, look lady, the thing is I just can't take it anymore," she replied. And she raised the cigarette to her mouth, taking a deep drag while she lit it.

"Artist, do you smoke?" Ana asked me.

"No, he watches," said Sonia, butting in. "We're the depraved ones, you and I. But for someone whose neurons already function properly . . ."

"But, not even a little puff?" she insisted.

I shook my head no. But at that moment, not really knowing why—perhaps to impress Ana—I heard myself say:

"All right, why not. But only out of anthropological curiosity."

I had never smoked anything, not even tobacco, so the first drag made me a little dizzy. But I didn't notice anything else.

"What?" they said in unison.

"But it's also . . . not a big deal," I retorted. And without thinking, I took another drag. Now that I'd started, I wanted to experience exactly what it was about hash that Sonia liked so much. And then, indeed, I started to notice something, though I didn't know quite what it was.

"Good," said Sonia, "because that's far too much for me alone. Marcos smoking. I'm going to go to the restroom, because I can't believe what I'm seeing. And order me another vodka with lime, please."

She grabbed the cigarette, took a long drag, and disappeared behind the pillar.

I spent a few minutes alone with Ana, and she asked about my research. I didn't take up too much of her time, but I told her about the trajectory of the internet cafés, how the line that I'd traced on the map almost matched the line of the ancient Arab city wall, and how one seemed to disappear in time in those places. I told her about all that and also mentioned what Montes had written to me in his last message.

"A hidden tragedy?" she replied, somewhat disgusted. "What the hell is this guy gonna pull? I'd be wary of him if I were you," she said, raising the cigarette to her lips.

I took a sip of Coca-Cola and, with a little remorse, I explained to her again that Montes's work sought to make people see what they didn't want to see. I told her that, for him, according to what I'd read, there was nothing hidden, that it was right there in front of our eyes, obscenely present, even though no one could see it.

"As if we were blind," she said, summing up, seeming now to have a clearer comprehension of what it was all about.

"Exactly," I said. "Just like in 'The Purloined Letter.'"

"What?"

"Yeah, the Poe story: the best way to hide something is to put it where everybody can see it," I said, reciting Montes's words from memory. "The most terrible things are right in front of our noses. That's what he wants me to look for here."

She sat there for a few moments, pensive.

"Something terrible and obvious," she started to say, " . . . something scandalous that we all look at, yet can't see . . . an injustice right out in the open . . . let's see," she took a deep drag of the hash and looked at the ceiling, as if she were trying to remember something. Christ . . . Wait, got it!" she exclaimed, "the illegals at the gas station."

"What's that?"

"At the gas station in the neighborhood around the train station, right by the highway exit." I nodded. "Every morning, a whole crowd of undocumented immigrants gather there, waiting for someone to stop by and pick them up for a day's work, or even for just an hour. It's a dreadful scene. And right where everyone can see it. Isn't that what your artist wants?" she asked me, somewhat sarcastically.

"Yes, yes," I replied. That's what he was looking for. But I didn't want to seem frivolous. So I expressed interest in that situation, beyond just my research for the project. Or at least that's what I tried to do: "And do people pick them up?" I asked, seeming concerned.

"Yeah, they're there because there are certainly guys who need their work. Some have already been hired and are waiting as if it were a bus stop, but the majority of them don't know if anyone is going to pick them up. I went to see it one morning, 'cause I didn't believe it could be true. I was shocked. A van arrived, the door opened, and people swarmed it like a bunch of lunatics. They pile as many in as they can. The driver didn't say a word to them. Not how much they'd be paid, not how many hours it was going to take, not where they'd be working, not even the type of work they'd be doing."

"And after that?"

"They pile in, go wherever they're taken, and do what they're told. Pick limes, work construction, pick melons, trim branches. Nothing fancy. Then they pay them shit, at most ten or fifteen euros for the entire day's work, and they come back happy as can be. Well, happy as can be is just a saying. They come back fucking beat. But at least they got a day's work. And it might take a few days before they get to climb back into another van."

While Ana was telling me this, Sonia returned from the restroom and sat back down with us. Ana offered her the joint, and she took a drag.

"And all that," said Ana, continuing her previous explanation, "right where everyone can see it. It's now just another part of the urban landscape. Like a park bench."

"What are you two talking about? The mystery man?"

"Yes," I replied. "I'm ruining Ana's night."

"Get out of here, artist. I'm thrilled to help you out. Thrilled, and you're going to invite me to the opening. I don't want to miss out on whatever this Montes is going to do." She took another drag on the joint—this time the cherry got so red that the whole thing almost went up in flames—then grabbed Sonia by the arm. "And now, honey, time to dance."

I stayed at the bar watching their purses while they went over to the small stage where the musicians were.

For a few moments, I thought about what Ana had said. Perhaps she had found what Montes was looking for. I wanted to stop by and check it out so I could tell him about it. I then thought about going over to the gas station early the next morning. I looked at my watch. It wasn't even one yet. If I didn't stay out too late, maybe I wouldn't have any problems catching the scene at the gas station.

When I went to set my glass on the bar, I noticed that they'd left behind a hash cigarette that had barely been smoked at all. Without thinking, I lit it and took a handful of puffs. Then I really started to feel a sort of haziness and I had to hold onto the bar for a little support. I looked around for Sonia and Ana. And when I saw them, I was completely entranced.

Sonia looked like she'd just stepped out of some Italian film from the fifties. Her movements reminded me of Silvana Mangano's in *Bitter Rice*. Curvy body, a swinging rhythm. And I noticed that I wasn't the only one at the bar who was dazzled by her dancing. If they only knew, I thought.

Then my eyes turned to Ana's body. And I sat there staring at her like someone looking at something very unusual. Compared to Sonia's curviness, she looked slender and light. It seemed like she was levitating. And Ghirlandaio's nymph immediately came to mind, the one that Aby Warburg had written so much about. There was something about her clothes that reminded me of the nymph's veil. It was the feeling that the veil reveals more than it hides. The thin fabric of her loose-fitting pants clung to her body, settling against her butt like some sort of external skin, undressing her from the outside.

I couldn't take my eyes off of this image. I was hypnotized. I assumed it was the effect of the hash. Her body, little by little, broke up into small pieces. And my eyes wanted to touch them. The shape of her nipples could be seen through her cotton T-shirt. I could feel their touch in my pupils. I completely disconnected from reality and could only see an infinite whiteness and two small protuberances. I imagined the tactile feeling of the cotton and felt a desire to caress her nipples through her T-shirt. Just a slight graze, nothing more. I wasn't even interested in what was behind the shirt. Just the contact of the shirt on her breasts. It was the sex appeal of the inorganic, the desire to touch the sense of touch itself. It wasn't the flesh or the cotton that were arousing me, but the contact between these two elements. And in this invisible interval of space, I lost all notion of time.

"Wake up, Marcos," said Sonia, suddenly shaking me out of it. "We're leaving."

"I'm coming, I'm coming," I said. And I returned, as best I could, to the real world.

As we left the bar, Sonia said that she was going to leave with Ana and that Ana would walk her home.

"You're the best friend I've got," she whispered in my ear as she hugged me tightly.

Ana also gave me a hug goodbye. Involuntarily, I grazed against her T-shirt and felt the firmness of her breasts.

When they left, I stood leaning against the wall for a moment and swore I would never smoke again. In the distance, I could see that Sonia, without a pause in her step, put her arm around Ana's waist and started kissing her neck. I imagined her erect nipples clearing a path between the cotton fibers of her T-shirt, sticking out, swelling, growing harder and harder. Once again I was overwhelmed by this image. And I returned home with it in my head.

I climbed into bed exhausted and fell asleep instantly.

5

When I woke up the next morning I had cottonmouth. My pillowcase was completely wet. You could have sworn that I'd been chewing on it all night. The image of Ana's T-shirt was still in my head, although it wasn't as hypnotic as it had been the night before.

I looked at my watch and realized that it was much too late to go to the gas station. Plus, it was Sunday. I assumed that wasn't the best day to go. So I put it off until the next day. And decided to finish the paper for my "Idea and Project" class, which was due that week.

I had to create a work of art, present it, and justify it theoretically. I'd been putting this off. I didn't want to be an artist, as I'd told Montes. But I had no choice but to turn something in if I didn't want to drop out of school. There was no way around it. I had to create something. And it had to be something clever. If I wanted to get a fellowship for grad school after I graduated, I had to keep getting the best grades. Something clever, I smiled at the thought. It was sad that something as small as a clever idea could be the difference between dropping out and graduating with honors.

I thought about my experience of the last few days. It might have been useful somehow. I was still fascinated by what I'd seen in the internet café. And Montes's last message to me was still swirling around in my brain.

Then I remembered that I still had an unused canvas from one of my classes on color. I looked around and soon found it, under a few layers of clothes. It wasn't too small—130cm by 97cm—and maybe I'd be able to use it for whatever might end up occurring to me.

I imagined creating something on that surface that could pass unnoticed even though it was there for everyone to see. At first, I thought of writing or painting something that was almost invisible, in white, something whose presence couldn't even be suspected. But then I realized that this would be closer to invisibility than this not-visible visuality that I was looking for. I thought for a few moments more. And then, finally, an idea occurred to me: a white canvas with a black line across it. A line that would be, in reality, a sentence written in such a way that it could pass unnoticed by the eyes of someone who didn't pay it much attention. It would be a way of playing with the ambiguity of the gaze and working with that which is in our field of vision but which we cannot see unless we pay close attention. A line that's actually a sentence. But what sentence? It couldn't be a mere statement to be read, rather, it had to be able to yield an action in response, something the viewer had to do for the work to make sense. I ran the idea through my head a number of times. And it finally occurred to me to write: "To experience this work artistically, you must call X phone number."

I imagined the result of this and formulated the issues that this piece brought forth. Three levels of interpretation. Some would simply see the piece as a traditional painting, a geometrical abstraction. Level one. Others would arrive at a deeper meaning when they realized that the line was a sentence. Perhaps they would crack a smile and see it as a conceptual joke. Level two. But there would also be others who would want to complete the artistic experience and would decide to make the phone call. The telephone number would be my cell, and I could strike up a conversation about art with anyone who called me. Everything would depend on the moment and the situation, so that each artistic experience would be different. Level three.

I liked the idea and decided to carry it out. For the class, I had to turn in a theoretical justification—in addition to the work itself—identifying the reasons for the piece, precedents, and sources of inspiration. I started with that. And I typed a number of pages in which I contextualized the work. I made use of Arthur Danto's theories about the art world and levels of reading and interpretation, as well as the levels of reading an image established by Panofsky: pre-iconographic, iconographic, and iconological. My piece, which didn't have a title, would be tied to those levels, but, at the same time, it intended to question them, since, from the start, those who saw the sentence and thought that it was just a line would already be interpreting something as something. Everything, at bottom, was a situation of "seeing as." Seeing one thing as another. The piece was going to be a game of displacement of the "seeing as," which only holds still and comes to a stop with the phone call. A call that would, however, contribute to the opening up of the experience. Of course, this was nothing new. I already knew that. Which is why I cited as a precedent the conceptual art of the late 70s. The linguistic and poetic conceptualism of Joseph Kosuth, Baldessari, Barry, and Weiner, but also the institutional conceptualism of Buren and Broodthaers. And, of course, the historical work of Valcárcel Medina, who combined the earlier conceptual experience with all of the levels.

Once I finished the justification, I felt like that alone was sufficient. I didn't think that it was necessary to create the piece itself. I had already thought of it, already had the idea, the theory, so why should I waste my time, strength, and materials on something that was easily comprehensible without even having to see it? This had been my soapbox issue with the professor of that course throughout the entire year, my belief that the creation of the work of art was unnecessary. Once it got to a certain point of conceptualization, for me, the reflections on the work of art were more important that its visual form. Nevertheless, he insisted that things had to be made in order for them to be thought about. And that the physical object had to be present for the experience to take place. Regardless of who was right, if I wanted to pass the class, I had no choice but to do what he said and turn in an artwork. So, begrudgingly, after having written a number of pages that I considered self-sufficient, I sat myself down in front of the canvas. First, I drew a line in pencil as a sort of guide. Then, with black acrylic and a pointed round paintbrush, from top to bottom, I slowly began to paint—to write, rather—the sentence. "To experience this work artistically, you must call this phone number: 67458807." As I slowly labored over each letter, I was fully aware of the senselessness and uselessness of it all. And not for a second did I cease to agree with what Lawrence Weiner had written in 1968: "The piece need not be built."

There was no reason to make the piece.

When I was finished, I stood back a few meters from the canvas and looked at it from that distance. And truly, it looked like a line. You had to get very close, almost touching your nose to the canvas, to notice that there was a sentence written there, and that that sentence requested an action.

To hide something in plain sight. To wait for someone to discover it. And, above all, to act on it. Perhaps that was what Montes was doing. Although there was a big difference: I hadn't wanted to get my hands dirty.

I didn't know how much longer it could stay that way.

6

I pulled up in my car to the gas station in the neighborhood by the train station. It was six in the morning and the sun hadn't yet risen. Ana hadn't exaggerated one bit: there were more than a hundred people in the lot next to the highway on-ramp. At first glance, I noticed that they were all men and all black. I soon found out that the majority of them were Sub-Saharan Africans, mainly from Mali, Nigeria, Cape Verde, and Senegal. And that there weren't any women there because no one would pick them up, at least not to go work in the fields. The bosses liked black men, and if they didn't speak Spanish, it was almost better that way, because they didn't complain or negotiate.

I stopped for a moment to get gas. It was the perfect excuse to see the situation up close. After I filled up the tank, I decided to go over and talk to someone, convinced that Montes was going to ask me about my experiences. "One testimony is worth more than a thousand statistics," I recalled, "a tear, more than a thousand reports."

I moved my Renault Laguna away from the gas pumps and off into a corner, near the air and water pumps, got out of the car, and started walking towards all the men.

What happened next caught me by surprise. A few seconds after I began walking over to them, more than a dozen immigrants were running towards me. I froze in my tracks. I thought they were charging at me. And I instinctively thought of running away. But they passed me at wide berth and didn't even look at me. When they got to my car, they surrounded it, opened the doors, and started getting in the car as best they could.

I soon realized what was happening. By the time I could get back to the car, they were already all inside. There were six in the back. I don't know how they did it, but the fact was that there they were, one on top of the other, crammed in there. Same with the front passenger seat, where there were two more. And even one in the driver's seat.

The only thing that occurred to me to do about it was start yelling at them:

"No, no, no! Please. It's a mistake. I don't have any work for you. I just want to talk."

But they didn't seem to understand me. No one got out of the car.

"Mistake, mistake. No work." I condensed my speech down to the minimal, while shaking my head no and gesticulating with my hands. "No money. No work. Out. Out."

They didn't respond and continued to try to close the doors. They looked at me in puzzlement, but none of them got out, not even the one sitting in the driver's seat, who had his arms crossed over his backpack.

It didn't make sense. Even if I had work to give them, how was I supposed to drive with someone in my seat? The key, for them, was certainly to get into the car any way they could. If there was any work at all to be had, they were already inside. If they'd achieved only that, it was still much more than those who were looking on from the outside.

I couldn't find a way to persuade anyone to get out of the car. So I decided to resign myself to the fact that they were in the car and wait until they tired of it. After a few minutes, which seemed like an eternity to me, a young man from the group still standing in the area next to the on-ramp—and who, this whole time, hadn't stopped watching the scene unfold—came over to me and said:

"You're not . . . going to start the car?"

"I don't have any work," I replied, gesticulating and trying to enunciate clearly. "It's a mistake. Mistake," I repeated.

"So why did you come here, then?" he insisted.

"Because I want to talk, I want to ask some questions."

"Questions? Why?"

"I want to know what's going on here, to know about you all."

"So, you don't have any work for them?" he asked, pointing at the inside of the car.

"No," I huffed. "That's what I'm trying to tell them."

"They don't understand. They're new. They don't speak Spanish."

Then I asked him if he could do me the favor of explaining the situation to them so they'd get out of my car. The young man looked at me for a moment with an expression I couldn't decipher, then addressed them in a language that I couldn't understand. Little by little they started to get out of the car, staring at me with looks of devastation on their faces, as if I'd created a situation of false hope.

"Thanks so much," I told the young man. And I took the opportunity to ask him: "Can I ask you a few questions?"

He turned around and kept on walking towards his friends. After a few seconds, as if he'd thought better of it, he turned around again and came back over to me.

"You ask questions . . . Do you pay?" he asked when he drew near me.

I thought about it for a few seconds. I hadn't talked about that with Montes, but I assumed that it wouldn't be a problem for him. And I told him that yes, if I was asking questions, I'd pay.

"Okay, then come soon. If no one hires me, you'll ask questions and pay. Agreed, friend?"

"Agreed."

As I shook his hand, the texture of his skin reminded me of the roughness of my hands after my clay sculpture class.

"By the way, my name is Marcos," I said before getting in the car. "What's your name?"

"I'll give you this one for free. My name is Omar."

It was still really early. The offices at the university weren't going to open until 8:30, so I couldn't yet turn in the piece for my "Idea and Project" class, which I had in the trunk of the car. So I decided to kill some time until then. I parked two blocks away and walked back to the bar that was right in front of the gas station. From there I'd be able to watch the scene carefully. I thought that, this way, I could take some photos for Montes and, at the same time, calmly observe the situation.

I ordered a *café con leche* and a chocolate croissant and sat at the table next to the window, as if I were at the movies, facing a screen that could save me from reality. During the time I was watching, four more vans stopped. The drivers didn't seem to say a word. Someone pulled up, got out of the van, and opened the doors. Then they'd wait for it to fill up, close the door, and pull away. Others made signals with their hands to indicate how many people they needed. Three, five, ten. Each time a vehicle arrived, the perpetual waiting turned into a mad rush. There didn't seem to be any sort of protocol at all. The first one to the car was the winner. It seemed like the whole thing consisted of waiting and running. Omar later corroborated this, saying that they'd tried to organize the thing a number of times, but it had always been in vain. No one knew if they were going to be there the next day. So it remained a matter of waiting and running. And if you got inside the vehicle, you had already achieved something.

While I observed the situation, I thought back on the scene in which I had been the protagonist. And I realized that, at bottom, I wasn't that different from all those who stopped to pick up the immigrants. "Out,

out of the car. No pay, no money, no work," I'd said, treating them like animals, making gestures at them the way you would with a dog or a horse. I'd looked at them like they were a herd, a shapeless mass of individuals fighting to get inside a car.

Then it occurred to me that my car almost functioned like a lifeboat for them, and that they all struggled to get in there as if it would save them from a shipwreck. Even though they were all on land, that lot near the highway, like this city, and like this country, was really territory in which they had all been shipwrecked. The ocean didn't disappear as soon as they got on dry land. It was at that moment that the power of the ocean truly gathered force. And my car, my Renault Laguna—I couldn't help but crack a smile when I noticed the paradox of the name, *laguna*, lagoon—represented to them a sort of lifeboat, as did all the other cars, trucks, and vans that pulled up to that place. Malevolent boats that were nothing more than another shipwreck, but which at least allowed them to stay afloat for another day.

I was submerged in these thoughts for over an hour. And during that whole time I never lost sight of Omar. I kept track of his clothes, rather than his face. A yellow cotton T-shirt with green stripes on the shoulders, an imitation of the Brazilian national soccer team jersey, a blue cap, and a red backpack on his back. The contrast between the colorful nature of his clothes and the darkness of the situation also seemed ironic to me.

Selfishly, I hoped that Omar wouldn't be successful in his attempts. I wanted his wait to be prolonged until

I arrived, for him to be there to answer my questions. In truth, what I hoped to do was the same as all the rest: employ him, make him work, get something out of him. At that moment, I felt like I was no better than the rest of them. But I consoled myself in knowing that it couldn't be any other way.

7

When I left for the university, it was 8:15 and Omar was still there. When I arrived at school, I ran into the professor to whom I had to turn in the project and I got delayed more than I'd expected, explaining why, for me, the piece was less important than the theory behind it. When I thought to check the time, it was already after ten o'clock, and I began to think that Omar must have already left with someone who had hired him to work.

Despite all that, I was hopeful as I returned to the gas station. The group had shrunk, but there were still more than twenty men there. They were now sitting in a corner of the lot, in the shade projected by the awning over the gas pumps, as if they were certain that something was going to show up.

It didn't take much effort to recognize the yellow T-shirt and the blue cap. Omar looked at me. And I noticed a certain satisfaction in his expression. At the end of the day, it was still work. And, as I'd promised him, I was going to pay him, although he didn't know how much.

"Twenty euros for the whole day," he replied when I asked him what he charged for a day's work.

"I can pay you that much for talking with me for a few hours."

"I'll talk," he said as he picked up his backpack and started to walk ahead of me before I could even tell him where we were going.

We walked into the same bar I'd been at before. When we sat down next to the window, Omar just stared out of it for a moment, as if it were the first time that he'd seen, from the outside, the scene he was usually a part of.

While I observed his lost gaze, I focused on his face. It was odd, I thought, this was the first time that I'd ever been face-to-face with a person of color. At least this close together. I could see the texture of his dark skin and was surprised at its radiance. The intensity of the color of his skin made the whites of his eyes seem fluorescent. His nose was wide, almost crushed flat, and his fleshy lips barely hid his large, somewhat yellowed teeth. But what caught my attention the most was the look in his eyes, subdued, yet full of strength and intelligence. I truly believed that I had discovered the real Omar in those eyes. I'd be able to recognize him again if I saw him on the street. He had ceased to be merely a hat and a T-shirt and had transformed into a face. A face and a name. Perhaps that is what makes us people, I thought. That others recognize us and know our names.

Omar ordered a glass of water, and I ordered a Diet Coke. I pulled out my MP3 player to record our conversation and a notebook in case there was any problem with the recording. Omar looked at me with some suspicion.

I started by asking him to tell me about himself. Where was he from, how did he get to this city, how long had he been here?

"Police?" he asked.

"No, don't worry. A friend of mine wants to know about you all. And your life could be important for him."

Then Omar started to speak. His Spanish wasn't perfect, yet it was fluent enough for me to follow without any problem.

He was twenty years old. And he had been in Spain for a year and a half. He was the oldest of six siblings and came from a tiny village near Ségou. This name meant nothing to me, but he told me that it was one of the most important cities in Mali, located on the banks of the Niger River.

To get to Spain, he first had to cross the Sahara, then the Strait of Gibraltar. In his country, there were a number of transportation networks that took immigrants across the desert. They were the same ones that offered guided tours during the tourist season. And they charged them much more than the tourists. He'd had to pay more money than he had earned so far in Spain in order to get a spot on one of the trucks that crossed the desert. And more still to get on a boat to cross the strait, at the risk of losing his life.

"It's more difficult to be here every day," he concluded. "But I'm not going back. Not worth effort."

He hadn't heard anything from his family for many months. He couldn't find a way to contact them. But, at any rate, he said he felt embarrassed when he talked to his father because he still hadn't earned enough money to send some home. He only made enough to get by.

"And why are you still here?" I asked.

"It's better to wait," he said.

And, at that moment, I thought that everything seemed to be reduced to waiting. Waiting for documents, waiting for work to arrive, waiting to go back home. They all waited, just like Omar at the gas station.

Then I asked him about the time he spent there waiting for someone to give him work. And he told me that he'd spent several months at that very spot. There were weeks when he didn't end up getting a single day's work. And others when he got lucky and worked up to four days in a week. But he had never brought home more than fifty euros per week. He had to live on that. At least he had enough to eat, he said.

Little by little, Omar told me his life story. It all seemed very interesting to me, but I was certain that this wasn't exactly what Montes was looking for. It was a sad life, a tragic one, but there was nothing in it that was different from the others. It helped give me an idea of the reality that took place everyday at the gas station. I could put a face on the people whom I had treated like a nameless mass. At least I knew the name of one of them, which was a first step. But I didn't know if that would be enough for Montes. Which is why I started to wrap up the interview.

"Why are you interested my life? Will you write?" he asked, curious about the reason behind all of that.

Then I told him, thinking that he wouldn't understand, that I was a visual arts student and that I was helping an artist who wanted to create a piece. His life could end up being part of a work of art.

"Art?" he asked, his face lighting up.

"That's what it's called, but . . ."

"I'm an artist," he interrupted. "I draw and write."

"What?" I asked, surprised.

"My story. I write my story. I draw important things in my life so I don't forget."

This changes everything, I thought. And I asked him about his work.

He told me that he was writing a journal about his life. With words and pictures, he added. While he was waiting around, he had time to write everything down in the half-used notebooks he found in trashcans, or on papers that people threw out and still had some blank space. He also found pens that were halfway used up. He had everything in his bag. It was all his worldly wealth. His only keepsakes.

"It's hard. I write in Bambara. My language is like art. But I can write in French, too. In my country I translate between the two."

That surprised me. How could someone like that spend day after day waiting around in the middle of nowhere? Omar seemed to notice my surprise and interpreted my look of disbelief.

"We aren't idiots, friend," he said, somewhat annoyed.

"I didn't say . . ."

"You all think," he said, not letting me finish, "that we don't speak Spanish and don't know anything, that we just sit there, as still as trees. But trees are wise," he declared.

I said I was sorry, and he accepted my apology, although I could sense some annoyance on his part. An irritation that vanished from his face as soon as I paid him his twenty euros. I took advantage of the moment to thank him and tell him that my friend would certainly want to see his journal.

"If you pay, you can see, no problem. I'm always in same place. If I'm not, it's either good thing or very bad."

When I said goodbye to Omar, I felt a singular emotion. I had finally found what I was looking for. I was sure of it. I had discovered something exceptional, which Montes would know how to appreciate. He had a story, but also an extraordinary piece of work.

That same day, when I thought it might be a sensible hour in New York, I called Montes at his studio. I couldn't endure the lag of e-mail, so I called him from the Sala de Arte. I was euphoric and, without a doubt, conveyed that feeling as I told him the story.

"This is the perfect material," he said in conclusion, after thanking me. Before hanging up, he told me: "Don't let him get away."

His words vibrated in the receiver of the phone for a few thousandths of a second, as if they meant something more than what was said.

III. CHOREOGRAPHY OF SHADOWS

1

I didn't receive any news from Montes until the following week. In the meantime, I worked on my exams and finished up the papers that I hadn't yet turned in. And I decided to do it at the Sala de Arte. The office was quieter than my apartment, the desk was bigger than the one in my bedroom, the chair was more comfortable, the internet was faster, and, above all, Helena was closer.

From my office I could just barely see her. A stack of catalogues, posters, and books impeded a clear view of her desk. But I could see her dark hair as she moved around the office and I could hear her shaky voice through the glass.

Tuesday morning, after she wrapped up a meeting with a local artist who was preparing an exhibition for the following year, Helena came by my office.

"Would you like to get a coffee?" she asked from the doorway.

I gladly accepted. I had barely spoken with her since Montes's visit. And I was anxious to tell her about the progress I'd made.

I couldn't wait until we got to the bar, before we left the Sala de Arte, I started to catch her up on everything. I told her about the information I'd sent along, the internet café, the gas station, and, most importantly, Omar, his extreme situation and his journal. When Helena heard about the journal, she opened her eyes wide and exclaimed:

"That's fantastic, Marcos. It's the perfect material."

I was surprised that she used the exact same words that Montes had employed. The perfect material.

"Yeah, perfect," I said. "But, more than anything, dreadful and terrible."

"Of course, of course," she said, amending her previous statement. "An everyday tragedy. That, above all else. But Montes will transform it into art and make it visible. Which is to say: truly visible. A story is nothing if nobody ever tells it," she said, opening the door to the bar and inviting me to enter first.

We sat at a table in the back. It was the time of day for a coffee break, and the commotion in the bar was considerable. So we had to sit very close in order to hear each other. So close I could smell her perfume. It didn't remind me of anything I'd ever smelled before. The proximity also allowed me to see some small wrinkles under her eyelids, which I'd never noticed before. I imagined that she probably didn't like them very much, but to me they were incredibly attractive. Same with her chapped lips, which she constantly moistened by gently running her tongue over them. In

142

my mind, I thought I could hear the infra-thin sound of that subtle contact.

I ordered a *café con leche* and toast. She, a coffee, black.

"I'm sleepy this morning," she said, arching her shoulders back and emitting a soft groan. "Ah, Marcos, that's such good news. The morning I've had today . . ." she again bit her lips. "You can't imagine how happy it makes me to know that at least the thing with Montes is going well."

"A lot of trouble with the exhibitions," I dared to ask.

"I wish it were just that. But no. It's the university. I sometimes wonder what I'm doing here, surrounded by incompetents who think that the whole college belongs to them because they have an office with their name on the door."

"You seem a little . . . heated."

"Aflame, I'd say . . . ready to explode," she huffed. "Once again they gave me a schedule they know doesn't work for me. They took away the class that I created last year. And then, finally, this morning I found out that, against the will of the students, it looks like I can't be the faculty marshal at your class's graduation."

"But . . . we chose you," I said, surprised. I remembered the class in which we all, unanimously, voted for Helena.

"It seems that, since I'm not a full-time professor, it's not possible. Anyway," she said after a few seconds, "that doesn't matter that much to me. One less responsibility. Plus, I don't really see the point of that sort of thing."

"It seems stupid to me, too. But the thing is that I was excited to be marshaled around by you, if only for a moment," I said jokingly. She smiled.

"Thanks, Marcos, truly. But it's just that sometimes I think that I should just do my work here at the Sala and that's it. It would save me a lot of annoyance."

"And we would lose the best professor we've had through the whole course of study."

She looked at me tenderly and touched my chin. It was the first time I'd ever felt her touch on my face.

"So you all . . . like my classes?"

"A lot, so much," I blurted out. I had wanted to express to her how much I'd learned from her, how fascinated I was with the artists she spoke of, all I'd discovered in the books she'd recommended. I'd wanted to let her know how passionate I was about it all. But I was only able to say: "A lot, so much." With a stupid look on my face.

"And I'd also like it *a lot, so much*, if all my students were like you."

I blushed, and she noticed. She smiled, looking me in the eyes, asked for the check, and, without giving me time to pull out my wallet, placed a twenty-euro note on the table.

Over the course of the week we went out a few more times for midmorning coffee breaks. She told me about her problems with the university and even consulted with me about the exhibitions that the Sala was organizing. For some reason, she trusted my judgment. And this trust slowly started to make an impression on me. I knew I didn't have a shot with her. But even so, I couldn't find a way to get her out of my head.

Whenever she was in her office, I couldn't help but pay attention to the conversations that Helena had with the artists who stopped by to present their portfolios and proposals. She listened to them attentively and treated them with respect, even when their work didn't fit the character of the Sala—or with what she wanted the Sala to be. But despite the respect given, some artists, when they heard Helena tell them no, dropped all pretense of politeness and let their frustrations loose on her.

Near the end of the week, I noticed that the volume of one of these meetings was increasing little by little, until finally the artist violently screamed:

"Fuck the character of this place. This is a public gallery. I pay my taxes and I have the right to exhibit my work here."

I couldn't hear any response from Helena.

"Got nothing to say? Who do I have to talk to? The government minister? With the president of the whole Autonomous Community? You'll see, you're gonna be sorry. And you can shove your fucking gallery up your ass." And he stormed out, slamming the door behind him.

When I heard the bang, I went over to my door, concerned. And there I found myself face to face with the artist, who stood staring at me for a few seconds.

"You're all sons of bitches here," he said to me. And then he marched down the hallway, yelling at everyone he passed.

Helena came out of her office and, upon seeing my stunned face, invited me in.

"Don't worry, Marcos," she said, utterly calm, as if that violent episode had nothing to do with her. "This is normal. You've got to have thick skin to deal with these people. They think they're the greatest artists in the world, the most sublime, and, as you saw, when you deny them something they believe belongs to them, they throw a fit and show you what they really are."

"That's no way to ask for something," I said.

Helena sat down and showed me the dossier. I started to leaf through it while I took my seat. It seemed to me like a second-rate Picasso.

"There are people," she said, "who have never cracked open a book in their whole life and then think they can reinvent the wheel. A transgressive painter, he calls himself. And says his work deserves to be exhibited because he has taken painting to an entirely new place."

I continued looking through the bound pages in the dossier. There was a sort of supposedly poetic introduction printed in a cursive font, as if it were a wedding invitation.

"The worst is that I'll end up having to swallow this bitter pill," she continued. "He'll go to the minister and then the president, or else the savings bank. And I'll eventually receive a call and then have to produce the most expensive catalogue—hardcover, with hundreds of pieces included—for him. Because people like him want to exhibit everything they've got in the gallery. These exhibitions end up being the most expensive ones of the year. You have no idea how much it annoys me."

"But I don't get it . . . you're the director."

"Yeah, but, as I said, sometimes you have to learn to swallow the bitter pill. There are things you don't like, yet you have to do in order to be able to do the things you like later on. For example, in order for Montes to exhibit here without anyone causing a fuss, I'll have to put up with more than one painter like that guy this year."

"Well, at least you have Montes. And that's much more than anyone else has achieved for a long time in this city. I wonder," I told her, "how you convinced him to do it."

"It's a mystery, no?" she said smiling. "Look, Montes and I have collaborated on more than one occasion. I worked as an assistant in a gallery in Madrid when he exhibited there for the first time. And . . . we became close," she said, after looking down at the ground for a moment, as if it embarrassed her. "Nothing serious, really. Montes is a very difficult person. But . . . I don't know why I'm telling you this."

"People tell me their stories sometimes. I think they see me dressed in black and think I'm a confessor."

"Well then I hope you know how to keep a secret like a priest. What I'm telling you stays between us, okay, Marcos?"

"A hidden noise," I replied. "Impregnable fragility." And, once again, without knowing quite why, I said something that I immediately regretted: "That whispered voice that caresses my ears will remain there forever and no one else will hear it."

What an idiotic thing to say. I pinched my thigh hard under the table to try to alleviate the shame. I had hoped to sound poetic and ended up sounding pathetic.

Helena smiled and said nothing. She just held my gaze for a moment, as if she were thinking about what I'd just said, and gently bit at her lips. I closed the dossier, which I still held in my hands, and put it back on her desk.

"Here's your provincial Picasso," I said ironically to ease the tension.

"We'll soon be seeing these awful paintings hanging on the gallery walls. And if not soon, someday."

We both laughed. And I left her office with a pain in my thigh from pinching it so hard and a single thought in my head: I'm an idiot.

2

The following Monday, I received an e-mail from Montes with a few ideas about the exhibition. Based on the information I had sent him and the data he had gathered, he was going to propose three installation pieces.

The first was going to try to reproduce the structure of impossible communication in the internet café. He sent me the plans and a sort of virtual reconstruction of what he was going to set up in the gallery. It had to do with the mirror play utilized by artists like Dan Graham. He was going to construct a sort of internet café booth and exhibit therein an immigrant having a video communication session with his family. The video camera would focus on the public instead of the immigrant, so that the immigrant's family would only be able to see the public, which, in turn, would have to look at the family as if they were in a fish bowl and observe the immigrant's frustrated attempt to communicate with them. It would be like creating an interruption of communication, he wrote, which would be reestablished every once in a while, at irregular intervals, but in a different manner every time. That way, the immigrant and his family would have to stay alert, because every two or three minutes, the image would appear again. But it would then be delayed for the amount of time it was offline. As such, synchronization of communication time would be impossible. And the messages transmitted would be tarnished and interrupted by the public.

There would be a sensor in the gallery that would activate the communication interference at the moment a visitor entered the space. The communication would be fluent only when the gallery was empty. Of course, the spectators wouldn't be aware of any of this, nor should they be informed of it in any way.

Montes suggested that I get in touch with some immigrants so that each day there would be one person doing a video chat session. They would be paid for a normal day's work. And, with luck, they'd have the opportunity to see their families.

The only thing that wasn't yet clear to him was the title. I suggested *Codex Interruptus*. And he didn't seem too displeased with it.

The second piece would also require my assistance. For this one, he did, indeed, already have a name, *Record of the Wait*, and it came out of the experience of the illegal immigrants at the gas station. He needed the information of each and every one of the immigrants who waited there over the course of a week. First name, last name, birthdate, skin color, weight, height, eye color, place of origin, profession, number of hours waited, number of hours they hoped to work, and actual hours worked. He would also need a personal item of clothing used during the day's work. With that information, he intended to create a sort of police record that would provide a reliable, textual account of an invisible reality.

There would be no photos identifying the immigrants. But the record would afterwards be turned into the police, thus reproducing the double standard of the policies of identification and control. "Everything has a dark side to it. The same policies that promote rights include, like a resident computer virus, elements of control and monitoring."

Visually, the work would consist of a series of foam board panels installed on the gallery wall one next to the other. Each one of them would contain the description of one immigrant, according to the identification records. A few meters away, in the middle of the installation, there would be a small pile of the immigrants' clothes, one from each of them, and an electrified chair in which the selected immigrant would sit. In imitation of a TV game show, Montes wanted to set up a game of sorts with the spectator, who, by sheer guessing, would try to match the items of clothes with the corresponding description. If they got it right—an improbable outcome—the immigrant who was sitting in the chair would receive 300 euros. If not, he'd receive a small electric shock. The immigrant would also be paid for sitting in the seat. And could end up with hundreds of euros in his pocket or hundreds of volts in his body.

The third piece would be the most difficult and would require the most care. He couldn't yet reveal anything about it to me. Not until he was absolutely certain of what he was going to do. The only thing I could know about it was that it would be centered on Omar. I was charged with tracking him down and telling him that we'd need his journal. Montes would personally work out the terms of the collaboration with him. And it was all to be prepared for his return on July 1st, only two weeks away.

The easiest part was to get people for the piece on the internet café. I spoke with the owner of My Land and made him aware of the situation. He told me that there wouldn't be any problem. The next day he gave me a list of names and contact numbers of all those who were willing to participate.

It was much more difficult to get the personal information of the immigrants at the gas station. Throughout the entire week I had to get there each day at 5:00 a.m., before the vans arrived, and try to ask the questions Montes had outlined. Omar served as my translator and explained the situation to them. He told them that they would be paid twenty euros for each record obtained. That was what they'd earn—the same amount they'd make for an entire day's work—just for telling me their height and weight, their first and last name, and how long they had been waiting there.

The majority of them didn't know how tall they were or what they weighed. So I brought a bathroom scale and a tape measure. At first it was absolute chaos, I was only able to jot down a few things and get out of there the best I could. But it all calmed down once they realized that this procedure would be repeated over the course of a few days and would become a simple routine.

With patience, I slowly filled out the records, which I had previously printed up like a proper form. After writing down the first name, last name, height, and weight, I'd hand them a piece of paper with a number on it, which they had to return to me on the last day of the week. On it, they were to write down the total number of hours worked and hours of waiting.

Even so, I sensed that it was all too confusing and that they weren't all completely aware of what they were doing. In fact, I assumed that the majority of them wouldn't understand any of it and would simply put down a random number. The only thing that really interested them was the twenty euros they could see coming to them at the end of the week when they delivered me the paper and an article of clothing they'd used during the week, a handkerchief, a sock, or even a sweaty pair of underwear. I envisioned the mountain of clothing on exhibit in the gallery as if it were a perverse version of Michelangelo Pistoletto's *Venus of the Rags*. Real rags, history's remains.

I finished it all up a week before Montes was set to arrive. I put all the papers in order and put them in a folder. Then I arranged a visit to Omar's house to have a look at the journal with Montes on the following Friday. I told him that the artist had considered publishing it—well, making it public, I wasn't lying—and that he would certainly pay him handsomely to borrow it. His face lit up.

3

I had sent Montes all the information he'd requested from me. Reports, transcripts of interviews, photographs, audio and video recordings. I'd done the best job I could. I eagerly awaited his return. But now I had to concentrate on studying for my exams. The one for Helena's class was, in fact, the most extensive. And I'd barely even given it a look. If there was someone I really didn't want to disappoint, it was her. So I spent the whole weekend shut away in my room, surrounded by books and class notes.

The exam was in a couple of days. I would have liked to stay shut up in my house, in the dim light and without any distractions. But the June heat was unbearable. The summer had started off strong and, without air conditioning, at certain times of day it was almost impossible to concentrate on anything. So I eventually decided to study at the Sala, protected by the artificial cold, no longer sweating, and, most importantly, without the fan blowing papers everywhere.

The afternoon before the exam, just as I was about to leave for home, I stopped into Helena's office for a moment to ask her how many slides she had ultimately decided to include on the exam. She was talking on the phone, but indicated with a slight movement of her head that I should take a seat. I did as she wanted and waited there for a few minutes. On her desk, full of catalogues and dossiers, my attention was drawn to a small black book with a title printed in typewriter font: *Design and Crime (and Other Diatribes)*. I picked it up, looking at Helena, and she gestured in approval, so I began to leaf through it.

Hal Foster. I knew of the author. Helena had made us photocopies of a few of his articles and, even though it took a lot of effort to follow them, I'd thought they were extraordinary. Among the best things I'd read about contemporary art.

"You interested in Foster?" she asked me as soon as she hung up the phone, before I could even get a look at the index.

"I love him," I replied. "The text you left for us at the copy center clarified so much about contemporary art for me."

"'The Return of the Real?'"

I nodded.

"Well, coincidentally, that piece has a lot to do with Montes. In fact, even though he doesn't mention him at any point, I believe that Foster has his work in mind throughout. He's received some criticism for not having included Montes in his list of artists."

"I didn't know about this one," I said, holding up the book.

"I think that's his most recent. The final chapter is a lesson in synthesis." I quickly searched for it and found the title of the last chapter: "This Funeral is for the Wrong Corpse."

"Strange title."

"It's a sort of cartography of where contemporary art will go after his death."

"What does he envision?"

"Well, basically, that the great stories have died off and that we are now left with different 'versions of living-on.' The spectral, the traumatic, the asynchronous, the incongruous. He ends up saying that contemporary art, in one way or another, revolves around these ideas."

"Interesting . . . Actually, the fact is that this would be perfect for the last part of the exam," I said after taking a peek at the images.

"I didn't have time to go into all that in class, but yes, it would certainly clarify quite a bit. Take it."

"Thanks so much," I replied. "But there's hardly enough time left before the exam is due. If it were in Spanish . . . but, well, it's in English . . ."

"Akal Press recently brought it out in translation, though I don't like their edition, I bought it just to have it. If you'd like . . ."

"In that case, if you don't mind . . ."

"Of course not. The only problem," she said, looking over at her shelves, "is that I don't have it here with me. But my place is nearby. When we finish up here, we'll head over there, and you can take it with you."

I thanked her and made to leave her office. As I crossed the threshold, I heard:

"By the way, Marcos, didn't you want something? We got caught up chatting about the book . . ."

"Right." I'd completely forgotten why I'd gone in there. "Ah, yes. It was nothing, just a really stupid question. Do you know how many slides are going to be on the final exam?"

"Privileged information . . ." I felt a little embarrassed. I didn't want her to think that I was taking advantage of our situation. "Mysterious mystery," she said, smiling.

When the workday ended, I accompanied Helena to her house. We rode together in the elevator, and while we were in there I started to get a little too nervous.

When we got to her floor, I followed her down the hallway and into her living room.

"Wait here a second, if you don't mind. I'm not entirely sure where I left it."

Helena went into one of the rooms, and I stayed there examining the living room. The house was small, but very inviting. The walls were lined with Ikea bookshelves and there were a few artworks hanging on the walls. I then noticed that they were only drawings and black and white photographs. No color disturbed the room's tepid, subdued color scheme. A black sofa, a glass side table, and a white coffee table in the middle of the room. It seemed like the whole place had been planned to be black and white.

The only things that gave the room a splash of color were the spines of the books that filled the bookshelves. I went over to them for a moment. And I only saw novels and poetry. I assumed the art books were somewhere else.

I've always thought that you could see a person's soul by looking at their library. At that moment I believed that I could sense Helena's soul.

"We share literary tastes," I said when I saw her come back with the book in hand.

"You don't say . . ."

"It's true. You have all four Bs."

"The four Bs?"

"Blanchot, Bataille, Beckett, and Bernhard."

"Aren't you really young to be into that stuff?"

"I don't think literature has an age."

"Well there are some authors that you have to read as a grown-up. Otherwise, they can be hazardous to your health. I discovered Bataille way too early and took it much too seriously. And you can't imagine where that led me."

I fell silent for a few seconds, examining her with my eyes.

"You don't want to know," she said, smiling.

"I'm doing fine with it," I noted. "Literature keeps me awake at night when I stay up all night reading. But it doesn't disturb me. I know where the limits are."

"And what do your classmates say about your reading? I doubt your professors are recommending those books. I suppose they're taking time away from your studies."

"Yeah, they do. But it doesn't matter to me. I spend the whole school year reading what I want. And at the end of the year, with a little extra push during final exams, I manage to come out all right. Using that method, I've never dipped below honors-level grades in any of my classes."

"Well, I don't know if that's going to work with me . . ." she said in a tone of voice that was halfway between seduction and challenge. "Don't think that just because we have coffee together, I loan you books, and you've come to my house, that I'm going to treat you any different than the others."

I looked at her, not quite knowing what to say. Then she walked over to me, caressed my face softly with both hands, and, standing on her tiptoes, gave me a kiss on the forehead.

I wasn't capable of understanding it. What did it mean? I didn't know how to react. And the only thing that occurred to me was to quickly thank her for the book and leave without thinking too much about it. She kissed me again, this time on the cheek, and wished me good luck on the exam.

"And, Marcos . . . don't over-think it. If you mix that book together with the cocktail of books you're putting in your head, lord knows what might come out of it."

Only after I'd closed the door did I start to become conscious of what had happened there. I thought through the situation over and over for a while. What did that kiss mean? Why had I skipped out of there so quickly? Then I thought that perhaps Helena, who doubtlessly knew that I had a crush on her, had wanted to make the situation even tenser, sensing, most likely, that nothing would happen. Maybe someone else in my place would have tried something, but I had chosen the easiest route. Getting out of there. I was a coward. I wasn't going to get another opportunity like that, I told myself as the elevator descended. What could I have done? I was convinced that Helena would never be attracted to someone like me. I imagined that if a professor wanted to sleep with a student, it wasn't going to be because she was fascinated with his intellect, rather, if it happened at all, it would be for his strong, youthful body. And I, of course, had nothing to offer in that regard. If Helena wanted knowledge, she had everything she might want all around her. Artists, writers, critics . . . I was a nobody. And if she wanted pure biology, ninety percent of my classmates were better candidates in that realm than I was.

Then I thought that the kiss on the forehead had dashed all of my hopes and set everything in its proper place. Instead of bringing anything closer together, that kiss demarcated a distance, as if she had wanted to make it clear that she knew what I wanted, that she accepted my admiration for her, but that nothing was ever going to happen between us, absolutely nothing. That's at least what I thought at that moment. And for some reason images from *Malena*, the Tornatore film, came to mind, and I couldn't help but identify with the young boy in love with Monica Bellucci. And I thought that Helena, like Malena, had simply been aware of her power over me and had wanted to assuage it with a kiss. A kiss that, nonetheless, had managed to shake me up inside.

4

That night, in my bedroom, I tried to concentrate on reading the Foster book and finishing up my notes for the exam. However, each of Foster's words were interrupted by Helena's breathy voice, her inscrutable gaze, or else the memory of her kiss on my forehead, a kiss that started to feel, little by little, like a physical, tangible pressure against my skin.

When I realized that I wasn't going to be able to find any way to concentrate, I turned out the light and lay down on the bed for a moment to get my head straight. There were too many things on the loose up there, floating around from one side to the other. Things that should be sorted out as soon as possible. In just two weeks my world had expanded greatly, and I had started frequenting places I had never imagined I'd set foot. That paradise that was the internet café, that hell that was the gas station, Montes, Omar . . . the images struggled against each other for headspace and advanced one after another, like a series of scenes edited together in no apparent order. But among all these, without a doubt, the image of Helena was the one that manifested its presence with greatest force. Her lips, her voice, the proximity to her over those few weeks, her scent, which was present in my room because of the book, the kiss on my forehead . . . these sensations managed to win out over Montes, Omar's life story, the conversation in the internet café, the immigrants sick with cancer . . . The series of images came to a halt for a moment and was reduced to Helena's kiss.

I reconstructed the moment once more. I sensed her touch on my forehead, again I heard the moist sound of her mouth as it left my skin, once more I felt her hands on my face. I reconstructed the whole thing from start to finish. But in my reconstruction, the maternal instinct that seemed to have motivated Helena' kiss was gone. Not anymore. That scene now took on a different meaning.

I let my imagination run wild and visualized those pale, chapped lips slowly descending from my forehead to my mouth. I imagined the wrinkled texture moving down along the profile of my face until it reached my lips. And at this moment I felt a thick, wet tongue enter my mouth.

I then noticed a forceful pressure in my pants. I pulled out my swollen cock and began to masturbate slowly. I imagined Helena asking me to sit down on the sofa and then straddling me. I saw myself pulling down the straps of her dress to reveal her breasts, caressing them gently and, later, sucking her nipples. I felt my hands lift up her dress, going under her panties, and tightly grabbing her ass. Then I saw her completely naked, kneeling in front of me, her face moving towards my cock. I moistened the palm of my hand and placed it atop my erection, imagining that Helena was putting it in her mouth. Next, I visualized her on top of me and I could feel myself gently penetrating her. I saw it all clearly, her arms raised, pulling her hair back, riding me while I grabbed her ass, sinking my fingers into her smooth, pale skin.

This scene continued for an indefinite amount of time until I ejaculated onto my own belly. I stayed there stretched out on the bed for a good while, not thinking of anything, as if time had stopped in its tracks.

On the day of the exam, I could barely look her in the eye. I focused on the task at hand and for two and a half hours I didn't look up from my papers. Although I couldn't get her out of my mind and her presence there was extremely distracting, I was able to analyze the slides she'd chosen to test us on with no problems. Malevich, Marcel Broodthaers, and Marina Abramovic. I knew it all. I wrote nonstop. I didn't want to disappoint Helena. My exam couldn't have been better. Paradoxically, when in the following week I found out that I'd received a perfect score and the highest grade in the class, it didn't matter that much to me. So much more had taken place by that point.

5

The graduation ceremony took place in the university auditorium. I didn't see much sense in the event and only agreed to attend at first because I thought that Helena was going to be our faculty marshal.

All the students' families had come, as if anyone there were actually going to graduate. Most of them still had years of classes to take. It was merely a symbolic act. Which is why I didn't even bother to tell my parents about it. It all seemed like an unnecessary performance to me. American films had done too much damage to the university imaginary.

The protocol for that afternoon included enduring speeches by the dean, the department chair, the male faculty marshal, the female faculty marshal, and the student speaker. After the speeches, the secretary of the college read off the names of each of the students so they could go up on stage to receive a diploma and white sash with the university seal on it. Once on stage, each student had to shake hands with the secretary, the marshals, and the other professors, then face the audience to receive applause and pose for the official graduation photographer.

One of the ideas that the graduation committee had come up with was for each student to choose a picture of a work of art that would be projected as they walked up to receive their sash. I hadn't been able to make my decision until the last possible minute. At first I thought of using Malevich's *Black Square*. However, as I left home, pissed off about the uncomfortable suit I had to wear, the fact that I couldn't find a shirt that fit, nor a tie that matched, angry that Helena wasn't able to be the faculty marshal and that I had to go through with this nonsensical act, I decided to get some minor revenge.

When the secretary said my name and I went up on stage, projected onto the more than six meter tall screen of the auditorium was an image of a foreground shot of Bob Flanagan's penis, nailed to a board and sliced through nearly to the base. I cracked a faint smile while my picture was taken and looked out defiantly at my classmates. Many of them couldn't believe what they were seeing. Not to mention their families. Parents, grandparents, siblings, boyfriends, girlfriends, small children . . . many of them had to look away, although the majority of them kept their eyes focused on the screen, as if nothing at all were being projected onto it, as if, in reality, they weren't actually looking at the obscene image right in front of their eyes.

It's possible that I had taken it a little too far. But at that moment it was the only pleasure left for me. Plus, aside from the pure provocation, there was another reason I had chosen the piece by Flanagan. I wanted Helena to take notice of me and realize what I was capable of doing. As such, when the image appeared on the screen and I turned to the audience, I looked straight at her, and she returned my gaze with a smile and an odd gesture that I was unable to decipher.

After the ceremony, there was a reception at one of the most expensive restaurants in the city. All the professors sat at a separate table. I ended up sitting next to some classmates with whom I had absolutely nothing in common and who also seemed somewhat bothered by the image that I had chosen for the ceremony.

"You took that a little too far, don't you think?" said one of them in an absolutely non-conciliatory tone.

"I thought it was quite normal," I said audaciously.

The tension was palpable. So they soon changed subjects, and everyone started talking about TV shows that I'd never seen and sharing stories and anecdotes about our time at college that I'd equally never heard about. As such, I decided to concentrate on my food and hope that the open bar would start as soon as possible so I could get up from the table and escape that situation. But it was all very drawn out. And the two hours I had to sit there seemed like an eternity. My suit was too tight all over and it bothered me throughout the whole affair. I felt that the evening was going terribly and that many of the jokes were veiled references to me. Which is why, in the end, so as not to be the only one at the table ordering Coca-Cola and thus calling more attention to myself, I started drinking the wine that had been poured into my glass. Every time I finished a glass, the waiter refilled it. And little by little I started to notice that my cheeks were turning red and that everything was taking on a new appearance.

When the open bar started and I had to get up on my feet, I realized that I was somewhat drunk. At that moment I wanted to go over to Helena, but I noticed that she was talking to another professor, and I didn't want to interrupt them. I decided to get in line to order a glass of something, anything. And there I found myself face to face with Navarro, who, according to what I had heard, never missed a graduation dinner for any reason.

"Hey, how are you?" he asked me, giving me a pat on the back. "You came without your friend Sonia today."

"As you can see," I said, looking away from him.

"The truth is," Navarro continued, seeming not to care that I wasn't paying much attention to him, "if you all came to class dressed the way you do at these dinners, I'd have to cancel more than one class midway through on account of a heart attack. Good god, the gals are all looking hot tonight."

He was trashed and seemed to be in his hunt-and-capture mode. So the conversation didn't last long.

"All right, see you around." And, without looking at me, he went over towards one of the female students who shot him a knowing look.

To me, this was the strangest aspect of Navarro's behavior, that it was actually successful. At that moment,

I wondered what it was about professors, who, even if they were, like Navarro, insufferable, unpleasant, and imbecilic, always ended up getting lucky. It must be the power. "A professor is a cock that can talk," I once overheard a conference speaker say. I smiled as I recalled the phrase. But I thought that there was some truth to it. There's a sex appeal in their supposed knowledge that ends up clouding one's vision.

Maybe that's what I felt with Helena. But my case was different, I thought. Helena was attractive, interesting, and had everything a man could want. It's true that perhaps I wouldn't have been drawn to her at first glance if she hadn't been my professor, but I was sure that at some point I still would've ended up head over heels for her. Just as I was at that very moment, when, emboldened by the alcohol, I managed to make my way over to her and I began to speak in a tone of voice I'd never taken with her.

"Well? Did you like the image I used?" I said, wrapping my arm around her waist. "It's moving, right? I want you to know I chose it in your honor."

"Well, thank you, Marcos," she replied without moving away from my arm.

"Yesterday I spent the whole night thinking about what artwork I should choose, and since I was also thinking about you all night, I finally decided: Bob Flanagan. I hoped that they were all nailed by it, the way I've been nailed by your image."

Helena smiled and said nothing.

"Well, then," I insisted, "did you like the image or not?"

"Well, yes, Marcos, of course. Why wouldn't I like it?"

And then I again repeated the same phrase: I hoped that they were all nailed by it, the way I've been nailed by her image. When she gave me a strange look, I said that what was happening was similar to what occurred in "Pierre Menard, Author of the Quixote," that I'd repeated the same thing because time had passed and now things were different, and, thus, the significance of the same action had changed.

"Even if only a minute has passed," I said, "with you, time is eternal, it stretches out, and I feel like I have to repeat things because I'm losing my balance and I no longer know where I am. Helena," I said, staring steadfastly at her, "you are my *tempus fugit*. And I would even escape time to be with you."

She smiled at me tenderly and gave me a kiss on the cheek.

"Marcos, I expect great things from you," she whispered in my ear.

I felt like the moment of the kiss on the cheek was being replayed and that this new kiss would only serve to put more distance between us. After such a thing, what could I do?

I got out of the situation as best I could. Looking down at my highball glass, which was almost half empty, I said:

"I'm going to grab another. Do you want something?"

"If you don't mind, I could really go for a Diet Coke."

I made my way back over to the bar. There was a line. I waited there for a few minutes and once again bumped into Navarro.

"I see you're getting very close to Helena. You making a pass at her?"

"No way, no way, we're talking about Montes."

"Ah, okay. Well I already told you once, be careful with Helena. There's a lot you don't know about her."

"Yes, yes, I remember, don't worry," I said to get him off my back.

"I'm being serious here. Not all that glitters is gold. She's a shady character. I won't say anything more. Now, of course, if what you really want is to fuck her, I can tell you how. You gotta pull her hair hard, shove your cock in her mouth, and choke her until she's out of breath. You'll see how much she likes it. That chick is a slut."

I couldn't bear it any longer and I grabbed him by the collar:

"I'm not going to let you talk like that," I screamed.

"Hey, all right, man, I was just trying to help you out," he said, shoving me away and straightening the lapels of his jacket. "Don't you ever come near me again. The only reason I'm not beating the shit out of you is because I'm bigger than you and you're drunk. Go to fucking hell, you and that slut Helena, and do whatever you please. But I hope you know that with that little innocent attitude you're never going to fuck her in your whole shitty life. Helena likes it rough. So, if you're going to hit somebody, why don't you hit her? Give her a couple of smacks and she'll be eating out of your hand. But don't you ever touch me again. Dumbfuck."

I turned around and walked away from Navarro. Fortunately, it seemed like no one had noticed the scuffle. With the music blasting at full volume and the darkness of the place, the dustup had just seemed like some strange dance.

I ordered a whiskey and Coke for myself and a Diet Coke for Helena, then went back over to give it to her. When I reached her, I found her talking to one of the models from the university.

"Thanks, Marcos. You know Francisco, right?"

"Of course, the model," I said in a somewhat condescending tone.

He looked at me, seemingly bothered by my presence, and then continued with what he was telling Helena. He said he was an aerobics instructor during the day and earned a little extra cash posing for visual arts students in the evening. Helena seemed interested in the conversation and in the secrets he had and sacrifices he had to make to keep his body in good shape. Rice cakes, protein, hours at the gym, wearing himself out every day.

"But you get the payoff too," said Helena. "I'm sure that when you see yourself in the mirror, you know that it's worth it."

"Without a doubt," he replied. And he kept going, saying that he'd always wanted to be an artist, but since he didn't have a talent for painting, he'd decided to be a model so that his body could play a role in art.

"And you haven't thought about becoming a performer?" I asked him, interrupting the connection they seemed to have formed in conversation.

"Becoming what?"

"A performer, making pieces of performance art. You don't have to know how to draw to be an artist. I don't know, but, for example, since you're so strong and prideful about your body, you could offer to let the visual arts students beat the shit out of you. An act of political resilience."

"What the fuck did you say?" he replied, visibly angry. "If anyone touches a single hair of mine, I'll beat their ass, man. I'm a peaceful person, but if anyone ever tries to step to me, I'll mix it up."

"Well, you're what we'd call a real pacifist," I said, specifying it for him.

"Ok, Marcos, that's enough," said Helena, intervening, affably taking me by the arm, "I think you've had too much to drink."

"Maybe so. But I'm going to grab another, because this one has really hit me . . . in the stomach." And I went back to the bar.

While I waited there, I noticed that Helena and the model were standing closer and closer to each other. He had taken off his jacket and started to show off his muscles through his tight shirt.

I didn't want to keep looking. When I turned my head their way again, the model was no longer there. Nor could I see Helena, who appeared behind me a few seconds later.

"Well, Marcos, have a great night," she said. "Watch that hangover. You've got to be ready for Montes tomorrow. You already know that he's arriving at the hotel in the afternoon. And stop thinking about it, okay? You're too young."

She gently took my chin in her hand and jokingly touched me on the nose. Then she turned around, threw a shiny black scarf over her shoulders, and walked to the door. I stayed there, leaning against one of the columns of the restaurant patio, watching her disappear into the darkness.

6

That night I hated Helena with all my might. I went into the restroom and stayed there for a good while looking at myself in the mirror. My incipient baldness, my gut, and my height weren't suitable weapons against the model's muscles. It was a lost battle. My army had nothing to do. I cursed my reflection and, meeting my gaze in the mirror, I thought at that moment that I would give all of my knowledge and intellectual capacities to have Francisco's body. There are times—I thought—when knowing how to speak, read, and write are absolutely useless. No one fucks another person's brain. What Eusebio Poncela's character says in *Martín (Hache)* is a lie. Well, when it comes to having coffee and talking about films, it's a different story. But in the moment of truth, what matters is nature, not culture. That's at least what I thought at times like those. And I then recalled *The Dying Animal*, the Philip Roth novel I'd recently read. In one scene, in which I saw myself reflected, Professor David Kepesh feels envious of the youthful, healthy bodies of the dancers who seduce Consuelo, the student he has fallen in love with. So the

174

dying animal imagines that he would trade all of his intelligence, all of his awards, and all of his books to be able to dance like them, to be able to physically seduce a woman, to be a strong, robust body. In some way, that night I felt like Kepesh, reducing everything to the most animalistic, rejecting my flabby, hunched body, and longing for the model's muscles. I wanted to trade all of my academic honors for a minute in that body. When it comes down to it, I then thought, knowledge and intelligence are merely strategies that some of us had to employ to make up for our biological lacking. The longest, most pathetic route. And, further, always frustrating. Because at the final moment, the most animalistic moment, when one has to sexually satisfy a woman, having read Heidegger and Derrida is utterly useless. Sex makes equals of us. In that moment, the only thing that matters is the body. And of course, on that field of play, Francisco's sculptured torso won by a landslide over my flabby, drooping belly, which nearly obstructed my view of my cock.

In front of the mirror, I saw myself as a dying animal at the early age of twenty-two. And I thought that what was happening to me was even worse than David Kepesh's case. The protagonist of Roth's novel recalls his youth and yearns for his erstwhile charms, vigor, and vitality. In fact, it's a book about nostalgia for something that was once possessed and then lost, about degradation and extinction. *The Dying Animal* was ultimately about old age and the loss of bodily strength.

For a moment I imagined myself as a proper adult and an old man, and thought that at that point I wouldn't even get to feel Kepesh's nostalgia. My body was young, but it was far from attractive. I would never be able to write memoirs full of sexual experiences and long for the days of my youth when my body was strong and robust. No. I was an old man at twenty-two. And the body had been forbidden to me.

At three in the morning they kicked us out of the restaurant. Those who had stuck around, including, of course, Navarro—who seemed finally to have found a female student who was game, and quite drunk as well—suggested that we should keep the night going at one of the clubs on the outskirts of town. In the state I was in—with a powerful headache, my tie in my pocket, the sleeves of my jacket rolled up, and shirttails untucked—I decided that my night was already coming to a close.

"Aw, man, don't back out, this is the last one," a classmate I didn't even recognize told me. By that time, he had certainly forgotten all about the bravado of the Flanagan image.

"The thing is I can't keep going, really. I can barely stay on my . . ."—I muttered, holding myself up against a wall.

"Come on, dude, we're all going to Le Moulin. They already reserved a spot for us on the guest list, which isn't easy at this time of night."

I finally let myself get talked into it and ended up in a taxi heading to one of the fashionable clubs in the city. During the ride from downtown to the area with all the nightlife, my dizziness and headache grew worse and I nearly vomited in the car. I had to open the window to get some fresh air and so that I could be reasonably awake when we got to the club.

I didn't dislike the place, which was decorated like a Parisian cabaret from the nineteenth century, imitating the Moulin Rouge from the film. But as I looked around, I realized that it wasn't my kind of place. It looked like a graduation party for a gym. Muscular bodies were nearly bursting out of white shirts buttoned only halfway up. The women also looked like they were out of some movie. Very long legs and very short skirts. Everyone was gyrating in spectacular fashion, and I was aware of the fact that I would never be remotely visible to them.

At the bar, I ordered my one-drink-minimum, another whiskey and Coke, and nearly finished it off in a single gulp. I didn't know who I was. The feeling of belonging to a world completely different from the one I was currently surrounded by swept over me. I looked around and thought that all those second-rate David Beckhams—who I imagined to be illiterate and brutish—were, nonetheless, much more attractive to Helena than I was. And again the image of Helena and the model appeared in my head. At that point, they were certainly at one or the other's house. I pictured them together in Helena's house, on the sofa I'd visualized during my onanistic episode. I imagined them in front of books by Thomas Bernhard, Samuel Beckett, and Maurice Blanchot. I imagined Francisco moving Cioran's *Anathemas and Admirations* off the coffee table so he could set down his cell phone and a box of condoms. I clearly saw him pulling down Helena's panties and searching for his own reflection in some mirror. A mirror like the one in front of me at that moment, right behind the bartender, partially obscured by whiskey bottles of brands I didn't know.

For a moment, and certainly due to my state of inebriation, the mirror in front of me, and the catroptical image that appeared in my head all began to blend together with the scene in *A Bar at the Folies-Bergère*, one of my favorite Manet paintings. In an atmosphere that was trying to evoke French bars from the *fin de siècle* of the nineteenth century, the connection almost seemed natural.

At the outset of our course, Helena herself had spoken to us about this painting in order to describe modern life as alienation. According to her, in the mirror in Manet's painting, two realities walked hand in hand, one imagined and the other real. The waitress who was the protagonist of the scene was split between the job she had in real life as a waitress, the space she physically occupied, and the mental space in which she found herself lost, the space she would like to occupy.

Everything was condensed in Manet's mirror, I thought, what we are and what we wish we were, and especially the idea of being completely alone in the middle of a crowd of people, which, as Helena suggested, was one of the central ideas of modernity. The waitress at the Folies Bergère was an example of this.

I stared at myself in the mirror and imagined that the waitress had transformed herself into a customer. And the person who was completely lost, divided, duplicated beyond the mere body, was me, with my head lost in the mirror.

I then looked at my watch. I thought a lot of time had passed, but it had only been ten minutes. I had immersed myself in my digressions and started to lose track of the notion of space as well. I noticed that, in such a state, time and mental associations seemed a lot like those in dreams. Places, ideas, moments . . . they marched forth with their very own temporality. And who knows, perhaps these were the true moments of enlightenment, these connections that one makes and then, the next day, with a pounding headache from the hangover, they all seem like idiocies, evocations completely out of place.

Together with the images of the Folies Bergère waitress, of the model looking in the mirror to watch his body penetrating Helena's, of the books by Cioran on the ground, of the shelves occupied by Blanchot, Beckett, and Bernhard, shocked as they watched the terrible scene, a feeling of dizziness suddenly washed over me and made me lose my balance. I grabbed onto one of the barstools next to me, but I couldn't keep myself from falling to the ground. Everyone else kept dancing as if it were nothing, without noticing my presence. I quickly stood up and sensed that the time had come for me to leave.

Leaning against a car in the parking lot of the club, I started to feel a bitter taste in my mouth, which was becoming more and more intense. I couldn't hold back the vomit this time, which splashed onto my shoes and pants. I raised my head, took in some air, and felt a little better. I then thought about taking a taxi back home. However, without quite knowing why, I decided to walk home to clear my head and to go by the stadium next to the river on the way. It was three minutes away from the club. I had heard Omar say that some of the Sub-Saharans played soccer there before going to the gas station. And I felt like taking a look at it. Montes would be back the next day and I needed to get everything that had happened out of my head and refocus my attention on the things that I still thought were worth a damn. I wanted to forget about Helena. And returning to Montes's world seemed like a good solution.

When I arrived at the lot next to the highway, I could barely see anything. But soon I made out some faint lights and heard the bounce of the ball. I didn't say anything. I merely sat down in a corner, my back against the wall of the stadium, and stayed there watching the figures dimly silhouetted in the darkness. Three on three. Flashlights demarcated the edges of the playing field. And the ball was almost impossible to see. They played in absolute silence. You could only hear the ball, the heavy breathing, and periodically a whisper. It seemed like some sort of nocturnal dance, a choreography of shadows. A beautiful image. Beautiful and horrible.

I closed my eyes and fell asleep to the sound of those intermittent whispers. It was the last thing I heard. Despite everything I had been through on that sad night, a sensation of momentary happiness invaded me. Dark, invisible, evanescent happiness.

IV. ICONOSTASIS

1

I woke up with an atrocious headache. It took some effort to open my eyes and as I stood up I had to hold onto the wall to avoid falling back on the ground. It was almost noon. I had just enough time to return home, shower, and get the smell of vomit off of me.

When I arrived at the hotel, Montes was already sitting in one of the chairs in the lobby. He was wearing the same long baggy black shirt from the time before and gray pants, which were tighter this time around. His shoes caught my attention once more, this time Moroccan-style black leather slippers with a point that twisted up into a spiral.

"I just came down," he said, greeting me with a handshake, his hand cold and apathetic.

How odd, I thought, that here I am face to face with him again and I'm just as impressed as if it were the first time. His presence had been constant during the intervening weeks. He had dominated my life from a distance. His e-mails had governed everything I'd said and done. I hadn't been able to get him out of my head at any point. And even so, when I saw him again,

I became even more nervous than the first time I'd met him in that very hotel.

"I've brought you something," he said, pulling an enormous book out of his bag. "It's the catalogue from the Shanghai Biennale. I thought it might be of interest to you. If you don't want it, I can just leave it here at the hotel. I don't plan on lugging it around again."

Of course I wanted it. I thanked him and told him that I didn't know that Shanghai had a biennale.

"There are biennales everywhere in the world. And the farther flung and stranger the place, the bigger the catalogue. Sometimes you have to bring a spare suitcase. For the catalogue and people's business cards."

"And is it worth it for an artist to make such a long trip?" I asked. And I immediately realized how naïve a question it was.

"Bank accounts don't care about big or small catalogues, places near or far. Plus, I'm going to tell you a secret: at bottom, everything is done for money. Art is the most important thing. But art is money. And that's the only reason. It seems like there's a lot of it in Shanghai. The rest . . ."—he fell silent for a few seconds—"isn't of much interest to me. At any rate, my piece didn't turn out too bad."

Montes took note of my incredulous expression and, altering his tone of voice, said:

"Sometimes you have to make sacrifices."

Then, after a short pause, he proceeded with what seemed to be of interest to him at that moment:

"And, speaking of sacrifices . . . we should get down to work on our thing. I don't have much time. Just a week. And by the time I leave, all the material should

184

be ready. So, let's go see that immigrant already," he said firmly, starting to walk towards the door.

The way he said the words "that immigrant" hit me like a projectile to the head. I thought about the power that word had acquired in his mouth, and, immediately, "immigrant" sounded like an immovable category.

"Omar," I said, specifying, "is expecting us this afternoon. We have to take the car to get to his place."

2

Montes barely said a word on the ride there. He looked out the window and observed the changing landscape, the outskirts of the city, the suburbs, and what remained of the fields, which had been slowly disappearing, devoured by urbanization and industrial zones.

Following the directions that Omar had given me, I tried to find my way, though not without certain difficulties. At the end of one of the highways that led out to the mountain, already quite a distance from the city, I spotted the bar where I had to make a left turn. Eight hundred meters later, in the middle of an orchard of lemon and orange trees, we came upon the house. Although perhaps "house" isn't the appropriate term. The dwelling was a sort of tool shed, no larger than twenty-five meters square, with no windows and a corrugated iron door that was off its hinges. In its place was a tattered curtain.

After I parked, Montes, without a word, got out of the car and headed towards the dwelling, walking resolutely. When he got to the door, he drew back the curtain and, in a solemn tone of voice that made me think of Jesus calling to his disciples, he said:

"Omar."

"No," replied a voice from inside.

I came over to the doorway of the house and took a look inside. There were eight men sitting on mattresses and listening to the radio. I didn't recognize any of them. For some reason, the scene from Ingres's *The Turkish Bath* came into my head, a throng of bodies in an impossible space, although here I found no trace of orientalist exoticism. Much to the contrary. It seemed as though I'd gone back in time. There was no humane way to live in that place. Of course, I thought, no one could call that a house. Much less a home.

"Fantastic," observed Montes. "I would love to reconstruct this house for the exhibition."

And as soon as he said this, he took a few steps back and looked at the structure as if he were a painter, making a square with his open palms through which he framed the scene.

"It's a box," he said.

In effect, the dimensions were almost those of a box. A coffin, I thought. A box of dead people. A large coffin full of bodies. A space that, instead of protecting, mortified.

While Montes walked around reflecting on possibilities for his piece, I began to look for Omar. I didn't recognize anyone inside the house. But the smell that emanated from it, a mix of sweat, dried urine, humidity, and heat, managed to make my stomach turn.

Then someone touched me on the shoulder.

"Good afternoon, friend."

Omar invited us to sit under the fig tree beside the thing they called a house.

"I already know who you are," he said, addressing Montes. "You're an artist."

"And you, a writer. Marcos has told me your story. I'm very interested in learning more about you. I want to make it so that everyone knows about your life and what it's like to live here."

"Yes. I want everyone to know problems."

Montes told him that he would like to exhibit his journal to show the living conditions of an immigrant.

"But the journal is in my language. No one here understands my language."

"It doesn't matter," replied Montes. "I prefer that no one understand it. That's not important. Plus, no matter how much they understand the words, they wouldn't understand much more. They wouldn't know what it is."

"So, what's the point if no one understands?"

I was asking myself the same question. What was the point in showing something that no one was going to understand?

Montes answered as if he were replying to Omar and me at the same time:

"The point is to make people aware of the impossibility of knowing. The opposite is actually even worse. If someone believes they know what the world is like, they won't take it upon themselves to find a solution. The equation is already solved. But it's much more problematic not to know, not to understand. That's the only way to react, when we know that we cannot know anything."

I wasn't exactly sure that Omar had completely understood Montes's explanation. Even so, he seemed convinced:

"Ok, friend, but you know that if you take journal, you pay fortune. Journal is my only treasure. I have nothing here. But I have this. This is my whole life."

Montes told him not to worry about the money. He would pay him what was needed.

"Friend, this is all my memories. It is important to me. You are buying my life."

"I'm buying your story," stated Montes.

When he said this, I thought that it wasn't entirely true and that, at bottom, he was indeed buying his life. The journal was the only vestige Omar had of that time period. Montes was going to take it and wasn't even considering translating it. He was interested in incomprehensibility. He was going to snatch that life away so he could exhibit it for some strangers. And no one would understand a thing.

When he offered him a thousand euros for the journal, Omar's face lit up. He didn't hesitate for a second. A thousand euros was a lot of money for someone in those conditions. But it's someone's entire life, I told myself. His only possession. Even so, Omar seemed to be sure about it.

"A thousand euros is good. I just ask that you take care of my story. Even though you don't know anything, my life is important."

"Don't worry, no one will take better care of it than I will," said Montes, cracking a smile. And then he asked him to show him the journal.

Omar led us back into the house. The smell of sweat that I'd noticed earlier returned with greater force. The men seated on the mattresses looked at us without interrupting the conversation between them. The Arabic music on the radio kept playing in the background.

"This money is important to live. I cannot escape here. This house and this life are like being in jail."

"And would you like to escape from here?" asked Montes.

"Go far away from here. Go back home with money. But I can't go back now. The money is much life for my family." He thought for a moment and added: "One life for others."

Montes heard Omar's words and, after giving a quick look around the inside of the house, whispered to me:

"I'm getting an idea for a piece right now. An absolutely masterful one. I'll tell you about it later."

Then he looked firmly at Omar and, again in a solemn and transcendent tone of voice, said to him:

"Omar, do you really want to leave here?"

"Of course, I want to leave."

"At all cost?"

He nodded.

"Even if you had to risk your life?"

"I already risked it . . . to come here."

"Well then, there is something that you could do to escape this prison. For now, I need the journal. We'll talk tomorrow."

Omar lifted up one of the mattresses and took from under it a small plastic bag that contained three blue cardboard folders filled with many different varieties of papers. Printer paper, pages of notebooks, receipts, letters . . . All of them with writing on the backside that looked, at first glance, like Arabic, but somewhat more geometrical.

"My life is in all these papers. There is a number on each sheet. A number is a day. Yesterday is the last one."

Montes took his wallet out of his pocket. It was chock-full of bills. I was surprised that anyone could carry around that much cash.

"One thousand euros for three folders worth of papers," he said, offering the cash to Omar. "I think it's a fair trade."

"Thanks, friend."

A thousand euros for a life. Without a doubt an unfair trade, I thought.

Montes took the folders from Omar. We said goodbye, and Montes told him that he should keep thinking about whether or not he wanted to leave there. And that he'd find him the next day to tell him how he could do it.

"A test," he declared. "A test of courage and resistance. You'll escape two times."

3

Helena arrived punctually at the restaurant. I didn't want to look her in the eyes, but it couldn't be avoided. And when I saw her face again, something writhed inside me. She greeted me as if nothing had happened. And hugged Montes as if years had passed since the last time they'd seen each other.

Even though I tried to act normal, I couldn't stop imagining her with the model. She'd probably been with him all day. When she kissed me on the cheek, I imagined for a moment that her mouth still smelled of Francisco's cock. She'd surely sucked it a few times. And now that mouth that had sunk as low as it could go was talking about art, as if it were nothing. Perhaps, I mused, that was the only way one could properly talk about art, with the aftertaste of the cock of a model who poses for painters in one's mouth.

"So, Jacobo, how's the work going?"

Montes showed her the journal and explained that he was thinking about exhibiting it. He told her that perhaps it would be better not to translate it because in that way it would create a feeling of incomprehensibility. And that he was probably going to take a few photos to display alongside the pages of the journal. Photos that would contextualize the writing. Although it wasn't very clear to him yet.

"What is indeed starting to become clear to me," he said, looking at me in search of a certain complicity, "is a new piece that occurred to me this afternoon. When I went into those immigrants' house, an image came to mind that I haven't been able to shake. The house looked like a box, a sort of container of people. And when I thought about how they all wanted to escape there and that such a thing was very difficult, I recalled Harry Houdini and saw those immigrants as some kind of frustrated escape artists, locked in a box from which they cannot leave."

From what I had read about Montes and the little I knew him, I could sense where this conversation was headed.

"I've imagined," he said, "a piece about magic and disenchantment with the world. As I contemplated that scene, I clearly envisioned a piece about escapism."

"I think I'm following you," said Helena. "But what form would it take?"

"Although I still need to sketch out a few details, I've been thinking about it all afternoon and I believe that it would be something like an escape-artist feat performed by an immigrant. Omar would be the best bet. It would be the perfect complement to the journal."

"The incomprehensibility of the text and the impossible action," she added.

"Precisely. What I've thought up is that we could enclose Omar in a box and submerge it in a tank of

193

water. Then he would have to try to free himself from the chains and get to the surface."

"It wouldn't be too dangerous?"

"Well, that's what the challenge consists of. It would be the performance that opens the exhibition. Afterwards, the box, the chains, and the tank of water would remain as remnants of the performance. Perhaps a video recording as well, although I'd have to think about that."

"That sounds fascinating to me," she said, visibly moved. "On top of the terror of the performance, it fits in perfectly with a tradition in the history of modern art. Some authors consider Houdini one of the first performance artists. There's more than one book out there that talks about Houdini's escape attempts as a metaphor for the desire to leave the oppressive and anguished world that emerges in modernity."

"*The Art of Escape*, by Adam Phillips," I blurted out. I had read that book and wanted to participate in the conversation as well. "The magician as liberator. It's a recurring metaphor of modernity. That's true. But the piece is too dangerous. And I don't know how much it would be worth it to run that risk."

"Of course, there would have to be some sort of test to ascertain his stamina," observed Montes. "But imagine it for a moment"—he made a gesture with his hands, as if he were opening up a movie screen. "It's a loaded performance, full of symbolic potential: the box, the confinement, the water, the sea, the chains, the oppression, the suffering, the escape attempt . . . I can't imagine anything with more poetry and political potential. Damien Hirst's shark in formaldehyde will be a sheer vulgarity next to this piece."

"Sure . . . if nothing happens," I insisted.

"The risk must be taken. What would our lives be without risk? And our art? I've put my life on the line time and again in my performance pieces. I've pushed my body to the limit. And it was always worth it."

"But it's one thing to put your body on the line and another thing entirely to put someone else's," I said, looking over at Helena who seemed surprised that I'd started to defend my position. I'd always kept quiet in front of Montes, and especially in these discussions, but at that moment I wanted to speak, I needed to say what I was thinking. And I didn't quite know if I wanted to do it because all of that was important to me and seemed dangerous or if, deep down, the only thing I wanted was to show Helena that I knew how to talk as well, that I was right there in front of her and I wasn't a mere observer.

"No one will be forced to do anything," answered Montes. "Tomorrow I'll make him the proposition. If he accepts it, I'll pay him more money than he would make in years working here."

"How will you do it?" asked Helena, interceding again, as if she wanted to bring Montes back to her territory and steer the conversation away from the ethical debate he'd entered into.

"I'm going to call my gallery owner in New York. I'm certain she'll be interested in producing the piece. She'll have no problem selling the remnants of the performance. I think six thousand euros will be more than enough for him. It's more than I've ever paid before. Six thousand euros or whatever he wants to get out of here. The key is that the metaphor be made real."

"Your art has always been about that, hasn't it?" asked Helena, so that Montes would continue along this line of thought.

"In some way. What I want, what I've always wanted, is to destroy abstraction and pure ideas and lead them to their full realization. To transform language into action."

"But language is just language, it's immaterial," I said.

"Never. Language creates reality. And sometimes you have to be literal so that this invisible reality can be seen. The metaphor of escape is only effective if it produces a real escape. Omar will escape from the tank as a metaphor of his escape from his real situation. And the money he makes will be used for a real escape."

"Only if he accepts the offer," I again insisted.

"Do you have any doubt? He sold us his story for less. He has sold us his past. Why wouldn't he do the same with his future?"

"Because it's his real life."

"But it's also his possibilities. Don't underestimate the power of desperation. You have no idea what we're capable of doing in order to escape the world."

The conversation dragged on, and for quite some time the conversation continued to revolve around magic, language, and metaphors. And it all seemed very stimulating to me. Much more than reality. In fact, I thought, that was the only thing I liked. Talking about those things, not carrying them out. And as I listened to Montes, I even began to think that I shared his beliefs, although it was never entirely clear to me whether it was necessary to take such risks in order to make a metaphor visible or give language material form.

I would soon have the opportunity to put it to the test. Montes was going to talk to Omar the following day. And, if he was willing, he was going to test his stamina.

"We should be sure that he is going to escape. The moment of escape will be like the moment of emergence in the works of Bill Viola, but with real content, not that empty spirituality that leads absolutely nowhere. I sincerely believe that this will be the most beautiful work of art I've ever created."

4

It was hard for me to get to sleep. I couldn't get Helena out of my head. It seemed that, deep down, she was the only thing that mattered to me. Whenever I had a free minute, I'd start imagining her with Francisco again. I felt like he was all men. Little wonder that he was a model. Pure abstraction. I didn't know a thing about his life. I had painted his body on occasion. His perfect body. But nothing more. I didn't know a thing about his life. Only that he had surely slept with more women than I could ever imagine. Another abstraction. The infinite number of women who had passed through Francisco's bed. An unimaginable number. And, among them, Helena, whose image I could indeed conjure up. A concrete, real, obscene image. That of her body penetrated by Francisco, time and again.

I wanted to masturbate to get all of those images out of my head and finally get to sleep. I tried, but my cock was flaccid. So I closed my eyes to bring the image of Helena right in front of me once more, the image of the Helena that I had fantasized about from the start. But nothing happened. Then I tried to think about something else. And I turned to Sonia. I'd masturbated dozens of times thinking of her. But that night I couldn't even make that work. I'd notice that I was starting to get hard. But then images of Helena and Francisco would immediately return, and my limp dick returned with them.

I needed to come. It was the only way to turn the page on this. It's sometimes necessary to ejaculate in order to exorcise demons, to take a weight off your shoulders. That was clear to me at that moment. I wanted to get Helena out of me. And I felt like the only way to do it was to yank her out through my semen. Then I thought about Montes. About the materiality of language and the necessity to turn abstractions and ideas into reality. Ejaculating to pull what's on the inside into the outside world. But also as if this extraction was, at bottom, an escape. As if I, too, wanted to get outside myself. And I thought that perhaps it was more about that than anything else. Not an attempt to expel Helena, but an attempt to expel myself from myself. I was the one I wanted to extract from my insides. It was my body that I couldn't stand. My flaccid, blubbery body. The flip side of Francisco's body. The accursed share.

I wanted to leave, escape that dark body, that obscene matter. Get out of the inside. Leap into the external. Escape. And then I imagined Omar in the tank, inside the box, trying to free himself. For a moment, I visualized Montes's artwork. Omar breaking his chains, opening the box, emerging from the water, as in the Bill Viola piece. And I saw his body, absolutely white, unpigmented, sterile, neutral, emerging as if it were a Christ resurrected to die once more.

Water, liquid, death, necessity of escape . . . While thinking about all this, I never stopped moving my hand up and down over my cock. And I began to feel it getting harder and harder. There was no sexuality in it. It was a physical act. The mind was a muscle. A muscle that had grown hard.

Right before I ejaculated, I thought of Helena. I held her image in my mind and didn't want to move it from there. I came on her face. In anger. The weight of my obscene body fell upon her eyes. And I could sense that something had ended forever.

5

In the morning, very early, I accompanied Montes to the gas station. He wanted to see with his own eyes what I had described to him many times via e-mail. He also wanted to meet with Omar straightaway and propose his plan.

I stayed in the car while he went to talk to him. From there, I saw Montes immediately recognize him. He didn't spend more than five minutes talking to him. And, judging from Omar's face and all his nodding, I intuited that he wasn't going to have to insist much. Montes handed him a paper upon which was written, I assume, the amount of money he'd receive for the performance and then he returned to the car with a satisfied look on his face.

"Just as I thought," he said as he got in the car, "it didn't take much to convince him. Money works miracles. It's the best argument."

"And he didn't say anything about the danger of the proposal?"

"Only that he didn't care what it might be, as long as he was getting that much money. Look at him," he said, pointing out the window. "With the situation he's in, for six thousand euros, he'd walk straight into hell if you asked him to."

I tried to pretend like I was pleased, even though, deep down, it really didn't sit well with me. It was a strange feeling. I was watching the creation of a true work of art, of the sort that had always interested me. There was something that kept me from being totally convinced but at any rate, I preferred to let it go. Surely I would understand it in the end. Plus, I didn't want him to suspect for a second that I didn't like what he was doing.

Almost before I could start the car, Montes started dialing a number on his phone.

"Good morning, Helena. Sorry for waking you so early. I had to call you. We've got our piece. He'll do it. No. He doesn't have any objections. Agreed. Yes. Something like that will be great. I'll await your call. Go back to sleep. We'll see each other later."

Helena seemed to have a location in mind for the performance to take place. It was one of the warehouses where they stored the artworks that belonged to the Community art fund. It was on the outskirts of town. She would call later with the address, and we'd meet there at noon.

6

After getting lost a number of times on narrow lanes that led nowhere, we managed to arrive at the warehouse via a minor roadway full of potholes and underbrush. No one was there. Not even a security guard. Just a rusty iron fence with small white snails all over it and some shrubs on the ground.

Helena arrived shortly thereafter.

"I've got the key," she said before getting out of her SUV.

She unlocked the padlock on the exterior door and then switched off the alarm.

"Nobody knows there's valuable stuff in here," she commented, "but it's best to be safe."

Then she opened the sliding door that led into the main storeroom. Metal shelves lined the walls from floor to ceiling. On them, covered with sheets, blankets, and plastic, one could discern artworks of every variety. It looked more like a cemetery than a warehouse. Although it also looked like a warehouse of failures. Of failed artworks. And all of them, covered in dust and rust, waiting to be hung or displayed somewhere.

"Only some of the pieces of art that belong to the Community art fund are stored here, the large format pieces," said Helena. "Even though, as you see, this place doesn't meet all the necessary conditions, there's also very little risk. These are pieces made from resistant materials. Steel, iron . . . many are outdoor pieces."

Montes remained silent and was constantly looking around, as if he'd been seduced by the place.

"Sometimes," Helena continued, "under some agreements, they buy too many things and then there's nowhere to put them. And they get stored here while they look for a place. Although, frankly, I would prefer them to be anywhere, in a government building, anywhere at all, instead of this place, collecting dust and deteriorating."

A few seconds later, Montes finally spoke:

"Perfect, Helena. It's the perfect spot. Surrounded by works of art that are no longer works of art but hope to someday become such once more."

Helena walked a little further, approaching the back wall of the storeroom. There was an enormous space back there that wasn't being used.

"This could be a good spot," she said, looking to Montes. "We'd barely have to move anything."

"It is, really. Yes. Perfect. There's space enough to put the big box in the middle and start the tests. There's also room for the camera."

Then Montes explained that he'd need a large box, something similar to what magicians use in their shows. And after looking around, something seemed to have caught his attention.

"Something like this." He pointed to a wooden box that contained a sculpture. A box approximately one meter high by a meter and a half wide, in which a person would fit with some difficulty. "Wait, wait . . . Can we empty that box?"

"I don't think it will be a problem," answered Helena.

"Now that I think of it, it would be best to use a box that has contained a work of art. The implications are much more powerful. Escaping from a box, escaping from art as well."

"Plus," continued Helena, as if she knew what Montes was going to say, "there are all the resonances with the 'white box' of the museum or gallery, juxtaposed with the yellow box that transports and stores things. The box that is never seen, that's removed from the scene when the exhibition begins. The visible and the invisible."

Montes gave Helena a look of complicity. And I noticed that there was an absolute understanding between the two of them. And, of course, I also understood the metaphor of the box. The art box as magic box.

"We're missing the chains and the tank full of water," said Montes.

"I don't think that will be too difficult to get. We can buy them in any magic shop. Or else we can certainly find them somewhere else. When do you need them by?"

"Now. As soon as possible. I want to start now. This can't wait. There's no way this can wait."

"Well, no matter how quickly we move on this, I think it will take at least a week to get those things."

205

"I can't wait that long," he responded, somewhat annoyed. "I can't wait at all. This has to start now . . . Now!" he screamed.

Helena fell silent, as if she didn't know what to say. I also kept quiet. It was the first time I'd ever seen Montes act like that. It seemed like impatience was consuming him from the inside out. It was as if he was already visualizing all of it in that space and couldn't wait to bring it into being.

"Okay," he said in a much more tranquil tone. "Perhaps I'll have to reformulate the performance . . . Perhaps he could start to do the initial test of stamina with this."

"The test?" asked Helena.

"Yes. To know of a certainty that he can get out. A piece about stamina. Close him up in the box for a few days to see if he really is capable of enduring it." He paused and stood there thinking for a moment. "Or, better yet, that could almost be the piece itself. Yes, that's better. Much better. That can be the piece."

"But that," I timidly began to say, "isn't what you initially thought of."

"And what does that matter?" he objected. Then, trying to argue his position, he added: "Works of art are modified by contact with reality. They are created little by little. And sometimes the final result has little to do with the initial idea. In fact, I think we should reformulate it entirely. Perhaps stamina is more productive than the escape attempt. Perhaps endurance functions as an escape. It's almost a contradiction, right? Remain inside as long as possible in order to escape for real. A sacrifice. Endure lack of water, lack of food, amidst a sea of excrement and urine. Oh, yes. Wonderful. Dreadful."

As he spoke of the project, he grew more and more excited. It seemed like everything was being formed in his mind and he could start to see it clearly in that moment. He then talked about a camera to record the process of endurance and the amount of time that Omar might end up inside there.

I started to think that it was all quite horrifying. But I stayed there, enduring Montes and Helena, as if I were also passing some sort of test of stamina.

Helena seemed thrilled with what Montes was saying and kept endlessly contextualizing his reflections within the contemporary art world, ceaselessly legitimizing Montes's arguments with the traditions of art history.

"The man closed up in the box," she said, "recorded in real time, like Andy Warhol's sleeping man, or his Empire State, but now without the glamour of Pop, but rather with the rawness of Montes's art."

"It will be perfect," he added. "We'll start with this, and then afterward we'll see if we want to do the piece with the tank of water or not. I like this idea of stamina. The test or the training for the piece itself. It will be like recording the process. The work itself can be the entire process. The recording, the box. And then the performance on the day of the opening. And the remnants of the performance will be left behind. It will be a self-referential work."

"And again . . . Bill Viola. The water, the shipwreck, the reference to origins and endings, like in his triptych."

"But . . . what about the other pieces?" I asked, thinking that there wouldn't be room for anything else if things went the way Montes wanted.

"The other pieces don't matter," he replied.

"But we have so much material," I insisted. "The internet café, the records . . ." I was thinking about all the things that had taken up several weeks of my life.

"It doesn't matter. Nothing else matters. We have to concentrate on this. Can't you see it? Can't you understand the significance of what we're creating? This right here, right now, is the piece."

I resignedly nodded my head. And he kept going:

"It's a great work of art. The others will be minor pieces. Maybe I'll make them someday. I have all the material. And I thank you for it. But right now we have to focus on this. Marcos," he said, looking at me with condescension, "this is how artworks are born, in the intensity of the moment. This is how everything is brought forth, when everything else no longer matters. When absolutely nothing else in this life matters to you. That is the true work of art, the one that blinds you, the one that doesn't allow you to think about anything else. And right now we are in the presence of true art."

"It's true, Marcos," said Helena, chiming in, "we're witnessing something big here. What is being conceived here is something you'll read about in art history books someday. And you'll be able to say: I was a part of all of it. I was there, and I saw how this piece was created."

"Further, it's the most sublime moment, the act of creation, the moment in which ideas emerge. Of course, then you have to carry out the action. But that's less important. Right now, without a doubt, we are experiencing the most exciting moment. Yes. Now . . . Now. Now I'm excited. Absolutely excited." And he looked over at Helena with desire. I saw it in his eyes. He would have penetrated her right then if I hadn't been there. Helena returned his look of arousal. The two of them stood there for a few seconds undressing each other with their eyes. I felt like a third wheel.

We left the warehouse, intending to return the next day to start the performance. Without saying goodbye to me, they both got into Helena's car. Which meant I would have to drive back alone. And I almost preferred it that way.

Before I pulled out of there, I saw Montes pounce on Helena, unbutton her blouse, and start licking her breasts. Then she climbed on top of him and started to move wildly. They didn't seem to care if I saw them. Without meaning to, I found myself face to face with Helena in the reflection of the side view mirror. Her eyes locked with mine. But I didn't feel anything. I stared at her for a few seconds, absolutely impassive. For some reason I felt quite indifferent to it all.

7

I spent the night thinking about everything Montes had said. I couldn't help but feel somewhat afraid. The piece was getting out of control. I slept a little, then woke up drenched in sweat, not knowing quite what I'd dreamt about. My jaw was sore from grinding my teeth all night. Something told me that it would be best to abandon it all as soon as possible.

Feeling uneasy, I arrived at Omar's house first thing in the morning. I had to pick him up and take him to the warehouse. Montes and Helena were waiting for us there, making all the preparations for the piece.

"Good morning, friend, I'm coming with you," said Omar as soon as he saw me. And he got in the car with his red backpack, stuffed completely full. He seemed to think that a long trip awaited him.

On the way, I talked to him about what was going to happen and told him that I wasn't entirely convinced by it. He didn't seem very convinced either. But it was a lot of money.

"I can escape forever with that much money."

I then told him that Montes was going to propose a test of stamina. I explained what it would more or less consist of. But he was still willing to do it.

"Doesn't matter. I'm locked in here anyway. And I don't make money. Anything is better than this."

"And your family?" I asked. "Do they know anything about what you're going to do?"

"They don't know anything," he admitted. "They also don't know other things. They don't know I live here, that it isn't even as good as doghouse. Yesterday I sent money. My family is happy if they don't know more."

"And your friends? Have they said anything to you? What's their opinion?"

"I don't have friends here, friend. We live together, but nobody knows anyone. Some disappear one day and don't come back. Every day there are new people. I haven't said anything. I don't want them to take my work. I don't want them to take my money. I work with the artist."

We kept talking for a good while as I drove out to the warehouse. Even though Omar said that he didn't care and that anything was better than living like that, I sensed that deep down he wasn't entirely on board. And then I thought that a person's dignity had to be placed above all else. There had to be something more than money, I told myself. But as I looked at Omar with his backpack on his knees, his haunting gaze staring out at the highway, not knowing exactly where he was heading, I realized that perhaps I was only thinking about dignity because money wasn't an issue for me. It became clear that only people who have enough money to live on can afford to worry about dignity.

We arrived at the industrial unit twenty minutes later. Helena's car was there, parked in the small courtyard beyond the rusty iron fence.

Everything was ready to go when we entered the warehouse. They had placed the box in the middle of the storeroom. And it was surrounded by a sort of film set. Next to the box was a large spotlight and video camera connected to a computer set up on a small folding table. The space had been completely altered. It was still the dirty, dark interior of an industrial unit, but the spotlight and the arrangement of objects around it seemed to have transformed it entirely. Perhaps it was because of the lighting, perhaps because of the presence of the box squarely in the center, or because of the camera, which imposed on everything a susceptibility to being perceived in a different way; I didn't know for certain, but the fact was that the space had been converted into something special and extraordinary. Or at least that's the way I perceived it.

I saw Montes next to the box, dressed in all black and concentrating on the preparations. When I started to approach him, a voice behind me warned:

"Don't bother him right now. The moments right before a piece are like a ritual for him."

Helena greeted me and introduced herself to Omar. She immediately led him over to the box and explained what was going to happen next. Montes scarcely even looked up at him, or even at me. He continued doing his thing and let Helena do the talking.

"I assume that Marcos has already caught you up to speed," she said. "It's very simple. What is going to take place here is a work of art, in which you will be the lead actor. So you understand, the piece is a lot like a test of endurance. You get in the box and stay in there for as long as you can. You'll have enough space, although, of course, you won't be comfortable. You won't have any water or food. You'll be able to breathe through a small hole in the box that allows for air circulation, although you also won't have much oxygen inside. In other words, just enough to breathe. Do you understand?"

Omar nodded as Helena spoke to him, but I wasn't sure that he'd understood everything.

"Of course, you'll also have to relieve yourself inside the box. This will complicate things further and make it more unpleasant. But that's the nature of the work. It will be an agonizing experience. If it were easy, it wouldn't be worth doing and, of course, there wouldn't be so much money at stake."

"The money," stressed Omar.

"The money, of course. Excuse me, I haven't finished telling you everything," Helena admitted. "The longer you stay inside, the more money you will earn. If you're able to last a week in there, you'll get six thousand euros. This is the list," she said, showing him a piece of paper. "The first day is five hundred euros, the second, a thousand, the third, fifteen hundred, the fourth, two thousand, the fifth, twenty-five hundred, the sixth, three thousand, and the seventh, the six thousand euros Montes told you about. Agreed?"

"Yes, six thousand," said Omar, as if that was the only amount that interested him.

"Six thousand . . . if you can last a whole week," insisted Helena, emphasizing the word "week," making sure that Omar had understood how it worked.

I was surprised that Omar was willing to do it. I thought that Montes must have been right. Sometimes money is the best argument. I just wanted to check that he had understood everything clearly and was willing to go through with it. So, in a tone of voice less inquisitive than Helena's, I asked him:

"Are you sure, Omar? Are you sure you want to do it?"

Omar nodded. Under Helena's surprised glare, I insisted:

"No one is forcing you."

And Helena replied to me:

"Don't worry, Marcos. He can get out of there any time he wants. He's not taking any sort of risk at all."

"But it's not the risk," I said. "It's that this is . . ."—I wondered whether I should say this in front of Omar—"degrading."

The expression on Helena's face changed immediately. And she shot me a violent glare of disapproval that I'd never seen in her before.

"Come on, Marcos, don't start with that right now. I don't think it's the right time to discuss what is or isn't degrading to people. Getting into a van to go work with absolutely no safety measures and being exploited for a pittance? Living in a filthy doghouse? You think this is more degrading? I don't think so. Plus, as you told him, no one is forcing him."

I didn't know how to answer that. So I just lowered my head to avoid the haughty gaze of Helena, who, without waiting for my reply, showed Omar some printed pages and told him:

"Here's the contract that waives all liability on our part and confers all rights to the images to Jacobo Montes. It also contains the amounts that you'll receive and how you'll be paid, in cash, so there will be no problem with the banks. No one will know you've received the money. No one will ask you to account for it. Think about it. As my . . . my friend has maintained," she said, looking over at me, "it's your decision."

"I don't have to think about anything. I want to do it now. I want money when it's over." And, glancing at me with a condescending look, he added: "It's not degrading at all. I'm choosing this because I need it and I want it."

8

Montes didn't even seem to be a part of the scene. He moved slowly from one side to the other, very slowly, but constantly, as if he were feeling restless for some reason. I'd never seen him so nervous. It must be the pre-performance ritual, I thought. I was somewhat surprised to see him like that. It's not that he'd been excessively friendly with me during our time together, but at least he had always maintained a certain level of cordiality. Now, however, he seemed like he was absent, outside of himself. And, paradoxically, I perceived that absence as a threatening presence, like a force that overwhelmed and paralyzed me. There was something about him that felt extremely unsettling.

Helena gestured slightly towards Montes with her head, and I understood her to mean that it was all about Omar's consent. The "yes, I want to" of the test. At that moment, in a solemn, forceful tone, Montes said:

"It all begins."

Helena asked Omar if he was ready, and he said he was. Montes went over to the box and closed the top.

Then he walked up to the camera, pushed a button, and said:

"Action."

And then, paradoxically, time seemed to stand completely still.

Everything was happening in slow motion. Montes went over to the box, walking deliberately, calmly, with a tranquility about him that had been entirely absent a few seconds earlier. He looked at it for a moment and, immediately thereafter, left the camera frame and started to walk over to Omar. When he got to where we stood, he didn't look at anyone but Omar. Not at Helena, not at me. And, besides, the look on his face had transformed into something else entirely. A dark, dangerous look that I had never before seen. A cold look, absolutely lacking in humanity, which managed to terrify me. Montes took Omar's hand and, without a word, led him towards the box, slowly entering into frame, or into what I thought must be the camera frame.

When they reached the box, Montes took his time in opening the top. He was acting like a magician, but without an audience. Unlike a magician, he didn't show the inside of the box to the camera. That didn't seem to be the important thing there. The importance of the ritual was imposed by Montes himself, with his rhythmic, unhurried movements. After opening the box, he made a gesture to Omar with his hand, indicating the path he should follow. The immigrant, who during this entire time had conducted himself with surprising naturalness and indifference, got into the box as if it were the most normal thing in the world.

Montes, without even looking inside, grabbed the top and closed it, careful and slow in this as well. Omar's head could still be seen for a moment, then his body disappeared completely. To fit the top on tight, Montes pressed it down hard until a loud snap was heard.

There were no iron chains, not even a lock. As Montes had said, Omar was free to get out at any point. There needn't be any obstacle. As such, the drama would be even greater. It wasn't impossible. It was a voluntary confinement. To be confined because you have chosen to be, although the choice was, of course, dictated by necessity.

At any rate, when the box was closed, I felt like some invisible force had placed it under lock and key, making the structure impenetrable. I then felt a strange sensation. The discomfort that I had gradually started to feel over those last few days came to the surface all at once. And I really began to doubt everything I was witnessing, the true meaning of the performance and the necessity of the confinement. I didn't doubt that all of it could be called art. That was of lesser importance. Perhaps it was art. It was in the same tradition of other artworks. And an artist was making it. It would be seen as art. Yet art was the least important issue. The truly important thing was this: what was the point of all that? Who would benefit? I asked myself. Omar? In some way, yes. Omar. But was taking that risk necessary? Was the degradation necessary? Was that whole ritual necessary? Without quite knowing why, all these questions emerged the moment the box was closed shut. Uncertainty appeared after everything had already been locked away, like a Pandora's box in reverse.

I looked at Helena, who seemed fascinated by what was taking place, I looked at Montes, who was still performing, I looked at the box, sensed Omar's body within it, and it occurred to me that perhaps he hadn't understood a thing. And it all felt repugnant to me. For the first time, I regretted being there. I had read about all those pieces. I had defended the theory, I had believed in it, the words had won me over. But now, when confronted with the reality of it, when I had to face it, when I had to put theory into practice, it no longer made any sense to me. The reality of it was too much for me and it made me nauseous. My stomach started to ache awfully, and I sensed a bitter taste in my mouth. But I was able to endure it without changing my facial expression, without opening my mouth, standing face-to-face with the scene, observing Helena and Montes with an expression that, now that I think about it, was no less frigid and empty than theirs.

After closing the lid on the box, Montes left the frame without even asking Omar if he was doing all right. He had closed the lid as if it were an automatic operation, moving one object to place it on top of another, with deliberate movements and an expressionless face, as if he were performing some sort of choreography. A choreography that, for a moment, reminded me of *Site*, the Robert Morris piece in which the artist moves a series of wooden boards around in order to uncover and then hide the naked body of Carolee Schneemann, reclining on a sofa as if she were Manet's *Olympia*. Morris, with a mask over his face, unemotional, moves from one spot to another, carrying out a task, meditating on industriousness and artistic exertion, on the relationship between art and work. *Site* intended to reflect on the place of art in the contemporary world. A place that, for Morris, was the same as every other sort of work. The North American artist wanted to resituate art in society. But what did Montes want? It was the first time that I'd asked myself that question. And I asked it almost as if I were a psychoanalyst: What does the other desire? I then realized, perhaps also for the first time, that I didn't have an answer. I didn't know what the other desired. I had never known. I didn't know what the other hoped for. Perhaps this was why it had all interested me so much, because from the start it had seemed like an enigma to me. Not only what Montes wanted at that very moment, but what his hopes were for his art. He had always maintained that he didn't want to say or show anything, that he only reproduced things. But that it wouldn't change anything, that he didn't want to change anything. Perhaps no one knew what he wanted because he didn't even know himself. How, then, could I aspire to know anything?

After a few minutes, Montes walked over to where we were standing. He seemed somewhat more relaxed, but his movements still retained their rhythmic nature, like someone coming out of an hour of meditation and slowly becoming acclimated to the real world once again.

"It has started," he noted, almost in a whisper. "The woodshed is partially buried, as Smithson said. The rest is out of my hands. Now is the time of waiting."

"What do we do now?" asked Helena.

"I'll stay here for the entirety of the action. I prefer to remain alone. I need to meditate on all of this. I need to experience the observation, the contemplation. It's best if you both leave."

"But . . ." Helena began to say.

"Don't worry. I prefer to be alone."

"Okay," she conceded. "If you want, Marcos can bring you something to eat tomorrow," she said, looking over at me.

"It's no problem," I replied. And exhaled in relief at knowing that I wouldn't have to spend the night there.

"Agreed," said Montes. "Tomorrow you can bring me something, although I don't know if I'll be hungry. The only thing I need is that you both leave right now. I'm getting the feeling that I'm losing my piece. It's nothing personal, but I need this moment of solitude."

"Ok, well . . . goodbye, then," said Helena. And I noted a little disappointment in her face. Perhaps she had thought that she'd be able to stay there with Montes, observing the performance and being a part of the piece. I felt a certain sense of satisfaction when I realized that he maintained some space that was off-limits to Helena and that, despite their close relationship, there were places she was forbidden to cross into. And it cheered me up to know this, perhaps because I thought that this way she would be able to experience what I felt all the time, that there were forbidden places, barriers that, for as invisible as they might have seemed, couldn't be crossed, no matter how close they were, no matter how weak they might have been.

As I left, I gave the box one last look. I imagined Omar inside and I couldn't stomach saying a word. I bid farewell to Helena with a simple gesture.

"Tomorrow I'll call you to tell you what time to come and what you should bring," she said. "I hope you get some rest today."

I looked at her without saying a word. Before getting into her car, she added:

"He knows what he's doing. Remember who he is. Jacobo Montes."

I gave her a look of agreement and got in my car. Jacobo Montes, I told myself. Remember who he is, I repeated. And suddenly the words of the critic who had been with Navarro at the Rrose Sélavy. "Watch out for Montes . . . he's the biggest son of a bitch on the face of the earth."

I started the car. The sound of the motor managed to quiet my confusion for the moment.

9

Once again, I couldn't sleep. I couldn't find a way to fall asleep. Without a doubt, it had all transformed into sheer madness. I felt like I had to stop it. For a moment, I wanted to put an end to it all. And I believed I could do it. I thought that it shouldn't be so hard; I just had to convince Montes. But then I realized that the easiest thing would be to abandon it all, make a clean break and have nothing more to do with any of it. Perhaps that was what I had to do.

I spent the night surfing the internet, searching for more information about Montes. I already practically knew his entire biography. I'd read much of what had been written about him. But I kept incessantly looking at websites, not quite knowing what I was looking for. Among the recent news items about him, I found some blog posts that discussed *Groundwork*, his most recent project, produced at the Shanghai Biennale. I had the catalogue he'd given me, but it contained only a few photos of the piece and a text that didn't explain very much. So I didn't understand what it consisted of until after I read the information I found on the internet.

Montes had worked with local artists on the subject of poverty in the Bund, Shanghai's financial district, where, next to all the enormous skyscrapers and high-end clothing boutiques, legions of indigent people live next to the buildings, as if the structures had been pile-driven into the earth from the sky and the poor people were just mounds of sand left over from the concrete. What Montes had done was a meditation on this metaphor. After doing some research on the real situation, for which he had local assistants—assistants like me, I thought—he had created an action piece with five hundred of the poverty-stricken people, whom he used to physically support a structure made of steel over the course of a week. Seven days, a number that seemed magical to Montes. "The days of the biblical creation," he said in an interview when asked about the length of the action piece. "God created the earth in a week. And rested on the seventh day. Today, however, there is no room for rest. They are seven days of hard labor." Paying them the minimum wage, almost as much as they could make begging for spare change, Montes had arranged for the workers to remain hidden in a sort of trench that had been dug into the earth by some backhoes. There they would hold up, as if they were human concrete, a steel structure that would temporarily house an Armani store, Armani being the very company that sponsored the piece. The impoverished people were allowed to work in shifts. But they always had to spend a certain number of hours holding up some of the weight, since, otherwise, the structure could fall and perhaps even crush them.

Most of the commentary about the piece was favorable. And there was hardly any criticism about the dubious ethics of the nature of the work and the way in which Montes degraded people. He defended his position saying that he "had visualized poverty by hiding it and removing it from plain view." He knew that it wasn't going to change the situation, but "it was a way of making the conflict visible and revealing the dark side of capitalism."

For the first time, I began to distrust what Montes said and took heed of other opinions that I hadn't considered before. What was happening there was serious. And I thought that what Montes was really doing was taking advantage of the situation. I then recalled his derogatory comments about Shanghai. That he worked for the money and that nothing else was of any interest to him. I compared that with his statements about political engagement and the dominant critical discourse, which legitimized that piece and other artworks by Montes, resorting to prominent leftist thinkers in order to claim that his art revealed the flaws in the system and endeavored to put them on display. And, in truth, I began to see that something was flawed there, not just the system, but Montes's art as well, which, in that instance, was financed by a company like Armani, whose image, on the one hand, was called into question through this game of banality by juxtaposing it with the poverty of the locale, but, on the other hand, by showing this self-critique, the company came out of it even more empowered. But above all, something was flawed there, because everyone benefitted from it except for the poor indigents, whose situation would still be the same a week later. And even if they came out of it with a little more money, they also came out of it as somewhat less of a human being, prostituted by the great artist.

10

Everything was silent. Nary a sound emanated from the box. Montes was still in the same place, sitting on a char, with a book in his hands that I immediately recognized. *The Tears of Eros.* Georges Bataille.

"No one ever finishes reading this book," he said without looking away from it. "The beauty of Chinese torture. These images disturbed me when I saw them in my youth and they have never completely left me."

When he looked at me, I noticed that his eyes were red and he had a different expression on his face. He obviously hadn't slept at all that night. But I noticed something more. He had the look of an absolutely deranged man.

"Are you okay?" I asked.

He gestured for me to be quiet and take a seat next to him.

"I've been thinking all night. I think I have to take this even further. The piece cannot be a half measure. You know? . . . An old friend of mine, Teresa Margolles, asked her best friend to give her the corpse of her stillborn child. In Mexico, it's sometimes more difficult to find a plot of land for the dead than for the living, especially, of course, if you don't have any money. So her friend gave her the corpse. So Teresa encased the corpse in a concrete block and exhibited it in a gallery. Nobody knew what it was until the concrete started to crack and the unbearable stench of decomposition began to emanate from it. I've been thinking about that piece since yesterday. While I read and reread Bataille, what I really had in my head was the piece by Margolles. I think about sacrifice and torture. And every time I look at the box, I think that perhaps it would be best to leave that immigrant in there forever."

I couldn't believe my ears. I interrupted his speech a number of times, arguing that what he was telling me was madness or, worse, murder.

"Madness? But . . . what is art? Art is pure madness. Why would someone make art if they weren't mad? And . . . murder? Maybe so. But what if murder were one of the fine arts? Haven't you read Thomas de Quincey? Plus, it wouldn't be a murder, but a sacrifice. Yes. A sacrifice. What is life worth compared to art? How many slaves had to die for us to enjoy the great works of the past? Art is full of sacrifices. Everything we see hanging on the walls of museums today is just the tip of the iceberg of something much more terrible. There is no document of culture that is not at the same time a document of barbarism"—he said, emphasizing the quote from Walter Benjamin, which I instantly recognized—"isn't that right? So this would be nothing new. What's more, the immigrant entered voluntarily. He's accepted his destiny. His life after this wouldn't be much better. He won't waltz right into paradise. Or do you think that the money he'll make is going to save him? That money is nothing. That money can't save a life. It doesn't solve anything. Sooner or later he'll have to die. And right now he's in the perfect place to do it. He's at risk. His life is pure risk. It's the same risk he took when he got on that raft to cross the strait. He could have died in the middle of the sea. Or die one of these days when he barely has anything to eat. Or die of some illness in the middle of that pigsty they call a house. He could die from any of those things and no one would remember him. Or he could die right here, right now and go into the history books. And be a part of a work of art."

What he was saying made some sense, but it was clear that this matter had gotten out of hand. Montes was absolutely out of his mind. As such, I worked up the courage and told him:

"This has gone too far. Do whatever you want. I'm not going to help you commit a crime, no matter how much you may call it art."

"I didn't say that anything was going to happen," he said, getting up out of his chair. "I'm just telling you what's been on my mind. But nothing more. No one is going to kill anyone here. I'm an artist, not a murderer."

Montes seemed to be taking back everything that he'd said. But he'd said it. Those were his true intentions, without a doubt. And now he saw his artwork in jeopardy so he was backpedaling.

I told him that, as far as I was concerned, he could do what he wanted, that I wasn't going to come between him and his art. But that I obviously didn't want to be a part of it.

"Good luck with your piece," I mumbled.

Montes didn't even look at me as I left the warehouse. He turned around and sat back down in his chair with the book on his lap.

Once I was out of there, I realized that, during the entire time I'd been in there, I hadn't heard a single noise of any sort from the box.

As soon as I arrived home, I called Helena. I told her what I'd seen and that I felt very uneasy about the whole thing. And, most importantly, I told her that I was quitting and that it had all gone too far for me. She had to understand, I was young and the pressure was too overwhelming for me. That's the excuse I used.

Helena encouraged me to continue with the project and told me that what I'd just told her must surely have been a product of my imagination.

"How can you think that Montes would do someone harm? Have you not understood anything that you've seen? It seems like, after so much reading, you finally arrived at the most trivial conclusion of all. Montes is not a murderer, and never was one. How can someone who has created such poetic works of art want someone to die?"

That's precisely what I had been thinking the whole time: How could someone whose art had, on occasion, been so revelatory end up doing or wanting to do what I'd heard him say that day? But one thing was certain. I didn't have a sliver of a doubt about what

I had witnessed. I'd seen Montes's eyes. I'd felt the violence in his gaze. His intentions were clear. And that was enough for me. So I told Helena that I couldn't be talked into it, that I'd already made my decision, and that I wasn't going to participate in whatever that situation might degenerate into. The next day I'd leave all the materials I still had, including her Hal Foster book, in her office.

Her tone of voice then became much more intense and severe. And the fragile, whispered texture of her voice disappeared completely for a few seconds.

"You're confusing things. I thought I'd found in you someone who could truly understand art. But it's clear that's not the case. Ultimately, there are very few of us who can rise to the challenge."

Silence followed. Then she continued:

"I just hope that, at the very least, you can retain the virtue of discretion and, since you are unable to follow the path required, you make a clean break of it and let everyone else work in peace. And if you're having morbid thoughts and it occurs to you to tell someone about them, then know that it would be best to just cast them aside."

"I'm not going to tell anyone," I said. "But I don't like this at all. And you shouldn't be a part of it. At any rate, I'm not going to convince you otherwise. I've already seen that you and Montes are very . . . come-patible."

Helena fell silent once more. I could hear her breathing on the other end of the line. Softening her earlier tone, she concluded by saying:

231

"Marcos, in all seriousness, what Montes is doing is art. And if you don't want to help, at least don't get in the way. Plus, I'm sure you've just misinterpreted things. But if this is your decision, then that's that. You're invited to the opening of the exhibition . . . just like anyone else."

11

Although I'd promised Helena I wouldn't tell anyone anything, I needed to vent to someone.

"Marcos, you caught me at a bad time, man," said Sonia when she answered the phone. "We're in intensive care."

"I'm sorry . . ."

"What's up?" she asked, without letting me finish.

"Nothing, nothing, it was nothing," I lied. "I just wanted to know how you're doing and how your dad is holding up."

"Well, terrible. Last night we brought him here with an infection. The doctors say that, since his immune system is already weak, his body probably won't be able to fight it off this time. God . . . and my mom is a wreck. She can't bear to see him with tubes coming out of him left and right. Today we were able to see him . . . Phew, Marcos, it's really rough. He's in that shape and still has a sense of humor. He told me he was an astronaut and that he was going to blast off into outer space, and that when he got to the moon he was going to look for the U.S. flag so he could take it out and replace it with the flag from his hometown . . . " She burst into tears and couldn't continue with her story.

"It's okay, Sonia, have hope," I said, attempting to console her. "You have to be strong right now."

It was obviously not the time to mention anything about Montes. So I said goodbye and told her I'd call her again soon.

"Thanks, Marcos. Truly, thank you so much for calling."

I felt guilty as soon as I hung up. I hadn't thought about her for days. I'd been focused on my own stuff and hadn't had time to think about anything else. I was still obsessed with Montes, and not even the conversation with Sonia had been able to rid me of those thoughts. So I tried to clear my head of all of it and forget about the matter. But, of course, it was impossible for me. Although I called Sonia more often over the next few days and even went to be with her in the ICU, Montes and Omar were still always on my mind. And the same questions were still there too, coming back to me again and again. Had he gotten out yet? Was he still there? Had Montes done something?

During those few days I kept searching the internet, going into all kinds of discussion boards and trying to find anything that had to do with Montes's extreme practices. Almost by chance, I ended up stumbling upon a discussion board in which people were accusing him of illegal practices. In one of his pieces about prostitution rings, more than one artist had even reported him for human trafficking. Following that lead, little by little, news items started to appear. In general, in the wake of any of his pieces, there would be a variety of indignant reactions. I had always thought that that sort of response only had to do with the harshness of the performances and with the incomprehensibility of what was done and exhibited. But now I was starting to see it from a different perspective. I gradually began to think that Montes, more than just a great artist, was, at bottom, a societal abuser.

I recalled Helena's words in one of our classes. "The artist can be a son of a bitch." At the time, I had been in complete agreement with this. The artist didn't have to be a good person. The fact that something was a work of art had no bearing on whether it was an action that was beneficial to society. That seemed clear. But up to that point, I had been omitting the second premise. The fact that art didn't necessarily have to be morally correct didn't mean that it had to be obligatorily evil.

What Montes did—and at that point it was clear to me—didn't cease to be art, perhaps even great art. I wasn't disputing that. But there was something more. And I couldn't drop it like it was no big deal. I had to act somehow. I had to take a position. I then thought that this was the problem, that nobody ever managed to take a position, that everyone preferred to remain silent, look the other way, turn their backs on the things they didn't like, and make excuses.

But there comes a time when you have to think for yourself. A time when you have to reflect, choose, and act. If it was clear that art and ethics were no longer the same thing, if I couldn't demand that Montes be a good person in order to be an artist, what I could do was make a decision and choose life over art.

That whole time, even though I was right in the middle of life, deep down I had always been on the side of art. The scales had always invariably tipped to the same side. I had thought that what Montes was doing was art, but that it ultimately never ceased to be life, because his work had the capacity to change people. I had believed that his art, for as much as it was presented in the form of transgression, violence, or abuse, was truly intended to change the world. That even what Montes said about it—that it was only possible to show and reproduce reality—was, in the end, a way to shed light on those things.

But now I was starting to realize that this wasn't the case. Montes didn't hope to change anything. His tautology—in which I had believed I could sense a vanishing point, a pathway beyond what was visible—was a simple repetition, a reproduction without difference.

What Montes was doing was, in the end, slinging shit at the world. I arrived at this conclusion after a few hours of reflection, during which I wrote my thoughts down on various sheets of paper. Sometimes it's necessary to be logical and reflective. Write everything down in order to clarify it and arrive at a conclusion. On that day, I had to write it down in order to become aware of it all. And the first thing I became aware of was my own naiveté. How could I have been so blind? So intelligent when it came to some things and so childish when it came to others. Anyone else in my position would have realized it from the beginning. But Montes had dazzled me, his art kept me from seeing what was underneath it all, his ideas had even worn down my very resistance. Sometimes things are hidden in plain sight. The more obvious they seem, the more difficult it is to notice them, as with Poe's purloined letter. That night, I was able—for the first time, I believe—to see the letter right in front of my eyes and finally listen to my thoughts. How could I have possibly held out for so long? I didn't quite know, but the truth was that that's what had happened. And now there was only one way out. I had to act. And now. I had already taken too long. I had to know exactly what was going on with Omar. I couldn't just make a clean break. So I decided to go see Montes face to face and demand that he put an end to it once and for all. I knew it wasn't going to be easy, but I had to try. This was my position. It had taken too long, but I had arrived at it. And I had to defend it.

12

It was six in the morning when I arrived at the warehouse. I couldn't let it go on any longer. I had tried to get some rest, but I couldn't fall asleep. Which is why I got there so early. I had to resolve this as soon as possible.

It was still dark out, and everything seemed absolutely gloomy to me. I was afraid, at every level. And for a few minutes I thought that it would be better to stay in the car until it was completely light outside. I even felt the temptation to turn around and go home. But I finally managed to control my stress, work up some courage, and go in there to set things straight.

I walked towards the warehouse, lighting my way with a flashlight, and rang the doorbell. I didn't hear anything. I waited a few seconds then loudly knocked on the door. I couldn't sense any movement inside. I waited some more. Everything remained silent. I then tried to open the door, but there was a padlock on it. I wanted to pick it the way they do in the movies, but I had never been good with locks, so I tried to open the door by sheer force, pushing and pulling back and forth to see if it would open. But it didn't work.

I thought about other ways in. The windows. There were no windowpanes in them, but they were too high to reach. I looked around, searching for something that might be useful to me, and I saw a number of wooden pallets stacked next to one of the walls. I thought that if I placed them one on top of the other, I might be able to reach high enough. I managed to make a structure from which the windows could be accessed with relative ease. Especially for someone who wasn't as clumsy as I was. Feeling the instability of the wood under my feet, I was able to climb up and stick my head in the window. I took my flashlight out of my bag and shined it into the storeroom. It was strange. At first it seemed like there were no signs of what had taken place there. No sign of Montes, the box, not even the empty space in the middle of the room. It couldn't be. It was as if there had never been anything there. It was inconceivable. And for a moment I thought that was enough, that I'd seen—or hadn't seen—what I was looking for and that, as such, the mission was complete. There was nothing there. It was all over. I could go home. Game over. A few moments later I reconsidered and decided that I needed to get a better look. If I was able to get that close, I should try to climb in and gain access to the interior of the storeroom.

I had to jump from the window to the floor. There were some cardboard boxes below that could break my fall. I knew I was going to regret jumping down. But I was going to regret it much more if I didn't get in there. So I ended up jumping. The boxes broke my fall a little bit, but not as much as I'd hoped. I landed on my feet and felt the full weight of my body on my ankles. I stayed there for a few seconds, stunned, holding my position like a gymnast, but not knowing if I would be able to move from there. When I took my first step, my whole body hurt and I had to sit down on the ground for a moment. Nothing was broken, but the pain was unbearable.

As best I could, I hobbled around, searching for the light switch. At least that worked. The storeroom lit up completely. And, truly, as I had seen from the window, everything had disappeared. Montes wasn't there, of course. But there was also no trace of the box, or of Omar, or the improvised film set which the warehouse had been transformed into. There wasn't even that big empty space that things leave behind when they disappear. There were no remnants of the performance, as if nothing had taken place there, or as if someone had made an effort to put everything back where it had been at first, all of it too clean, too similar to the first time we went in there.

I pondered the situation for a few seconds. Five days had passed, almost six, since Omar had entered the box. The week that he was willing to endure in the box still wasn't over. So the performance should still have been ongoing, unless, of course, something had gone wrong. Plus, the warehouse seemed like it had been in that state for more than one day. You didn't have to be Sherlock Holmes to understand that things accumulate a certain amount of dust and you can tell when they've been moved.

For a moment, I even began to think that nothing had ever been moved around in there, that it had all been a figment of my imagination, and that I was the one who had created the whole debacle in my head. I even doubted Montes's existence.

Imagining the worst, I looked for traces of blood or some indication that Montes had tried to carry out what he had wanted to do. If there was no one in the warehouse, only two things could have happened: either Omar had left the box early or Montes had kept his word.

Although the only obvious thing was that no one was there. And, above all, that I had arrived too late.

I had arrived too late. And yet it was still too early to try to look for Omar somewhere else. And then I thought of the gas station. Perhaps someone had information about him.

There were still a lot of immigrants in the lot when I arrived. It was the time of day with the heaviest van traffic and there was a lot of commotion. I glanced around, trying to find Omar, but I didn't see him. I was no longer just looking for his hat and T-shirt. I was looking for his face; I remembered it perfectly. I asked a few men, but no one could tell me anything. I recognized one of his companions by his clothing—in this case, yes, just by his clothing—or at least someone I'd seen him talk to on occasion. I went over to him and asked him if he'd seen Omar. He remembered me, the artist's friend. And no, he didn't know anything about Omar. Just that he'd never come back to the gas station.

"But I'm not surprised," he said. "A lot of people come one day and we never see them again."

He also told me that there were no goodbyes and that people who got into a truck or a van never looked back. To make it into a van, you had to hustle and you couldn't make any concessions. There were no goodbyes. Not at all. There were also no goodbyes for people who were leaving or people who were never coming back. They simply saw them no more. Like Omar, who wasn't there anymore. But also like many others, who at a certain time just stopped showing up. Nothing strange. It was like that. One day you're there and the next you're not. And no one asks where you've gone. Omar seemed to have joined the list of those who'd left. Plus, he had a little something when he left. Many others leave and have nothing. They simply stop being there. You hope that they've found something better. Or that they've simply found something.

13

When I arrived at Omar's house, the door—the curtain—was open. It seemed obvious that no one was going to rob people who had nothing. I poked my head inside and smelled the same scent of sweat I had the first time. But no one was there. I remembered where Omar had sat, the corner that belonged to him and the mattress underneath which he kept his journal. It was now covered with clothes and other things.

I wasn't going to leave until someone I could ask questions of arrived. So I decided to sit down and wait, on a mattress with no sheets, which was torn up in the middle and covered in sweat and urine stains. In the shadows of that concrete prison, I thought, for the first time, that perhaps Omar had found something better. The most logical possibility was that he'd left. Perhaps he hadn't made it the full seven days, but with two or three thousand euros he would have been able to leave Montes's box and also escape that doghouse. Maybe the escape had been made. But even so, if he had really left the box and earned the money Montes had offered him, that didn't change things much. Omar was one person among millions. It changed nothing. The others were still at the gas station and that house was still a prison. Whoever it was that had taken Omar's mattress was still in the same place. None of it changed anything.

I thought, however, that it was possible that Montes had something of a point. Because if Omar had managed to leave that place, something had changed. It wasn't much, very little indeed, almost nothing. But it was a life, changed momentarily. Something minimal, something that wouldn't last forever. But, in the end, something. At that moment a poem by Bertolt Brecht popped into my head, which Montes had used as a source of inspiration for one of his pieces and which was etched in my memory:

I hear that in New York,
At the corner of 26th Street and Broadway,
A man stands every evening during the winter months
And gets beds for the homeless there
By appealing to passers-by.

It won't change the world,
It won't improve relations among men
It will not shorten the age of exploitation
But a few men have a bed for the night
For a night the wind is kept from them
The snow meant for them falls on the roadway.

Montes had said on more than one occasion that all he did was reproduce the world. But I had believed that something deep down was changed, that in this repetition there was change, and that though "it will not shorten the age of exploitation . . . a few men have a bed for the night." However, after giving it careful thought, that afternoon I reached the conclusion that the only one who had a bed was the artist himself. No one went anywhere, they weren't kept safe for the night, just the artist himself. He was the only one who kept his distance, the only one who managed to not get burned by reality. Because even in the pieces where he risked his own body, Montes was aware of the space he occupied. And this knowledge of his location was what allowed him to be saved.

I then imagined that it was all a sort of iconostasis. I knew from my art history classes that in Byzantine churches they had popularized the use of this architectural element, a sort of latticework barrier that separated the faithful from the space occupied by the priest during the celebration of the Eucharist. This structure, which could be made of wood or even stone, was particularly useful during the consecration of the host, when the bread and wine are transformed into the body and blood of Christ and the truly mysterious moment of the mass takes place, the transubstantiation, the transformation of the substance into the sacred. It was at that numinous moment when the iconostasis, which separated the faithful from the divine light, made the most sense. The *stasis* created a respectful distance from the sacred, but it also preserved the equilibrium between the two points, keeping them static and at rest. And thus it saved the faithful from the dangers of the sacred image, too excessively pure and true to be seen by the eyes of sinners.

Some theories about the iconostasis held that this element was a metaphor for the fusion of the sacred and the divine. But I had always thought that it was a filter, a sort of screen that served almost as a pair of sunglasses, allowing some light through, but not all of it. The iconostasis, therefore, as a space of mediation, but also as a space in which proper distance was maintained, a liminal veil between the sacred and the profane.

I had never seen it written in reference to Montes's work. Nobody had seemed to notice, but I was sure that his art, at bottom, had to something to do with this question, with the attempt to rend or shatter the iconostasis. This method of transforming art into life was an attempt to get rid of the iconostasis, to bring into contact the most sacred with the most mundane. However, on second thought, Montes's art had never been able to completely eliminate that veil. Because, in reality, the artist himself was the iconostasis. Because the body and mind of the artist functioned as the screen, the veil covering life. And it kept him protected. Him and no one else. Because there was no protection for all the other people he used. They saw pure reality. There was no iconostasis for Omar, nor for the countless others who were risking their lives. Art was useless for them. And, nevertheless, the iconostasis could never disappear for Montes. It was written upon his body. It was his wound, but also his armor. That which he hoped to destroy, but also that which kept him alive.

I thought about all this as I sat on the torn-up, sweaty mattress that had once belonged to Omar. I waited there until noon when the inhabitants of that prison began to arrive and, one by one, they all confirmed that they had no news about Omar. They didn't see the problem. He had left and that was that. He had left his bicycle, and the others were already using it.

Before I left, I tried to call Montes a number of times. I felt the need to do it. Only he or Helena would know what had really happened at the warehouse. But no one picked up. I got a voicemail message in English and didn't know what to say. Helena didn't answer either. At first her phone rang and rang. Then it seemed like it had been turned off or wasn't getting service. I thought about turning to the police. But what would I tell them? I had nothing. An immigrant had disappeared. So what? He was already invisible before he disappeared. He had never really existed in the eyes of the law. I assumed that no one would take the case seriously. Plus, at bottom—and perhaps this was the determining factor—I didn't really want to get involved with that mess. I had done all I could do. I had taken a position. And at that moment I thought that was enough. Even though, in reality, it was completely useless.

14

I rang the doorbell and waited for a moment. When you make a phone call, it's easy for someone to ignore you. But one's physical presence is more difficult to avoid. Even in this day and age, the body is still unavoidable. Perhaps for that reason Helena had no other choice but to open her door.

"I know what it is you want to know," she said before greeting me. "Come in, I'll explain." She led me over to the living room and gestured for me to have a seat on the sofa.

I told her that I'd been inside the warehouse and that everything was gone. And that I went looking for Omar in a few different places and hadn't found a trace of him anywhere.

"I can imagine what you're thinking. But it's all much simpler than that, Marcos. Omar decided to get out, on the day after you abandoned the project, as a matter of fact. He couldn't take it anymore. It was hard to be inside there."

"And why hasn't anyone heard from him?"

"Because he decided to leave. He made some money—not as much as he would have made if he'd held out until the end, but much more than he could have earned from many weeks of work."

"Okay . . . but people don't just disappear like that, from one day to the next."

"Oh, don't they? People disappear every day. You yourself said that that was no way to live and that people were always coming and going. They disappear and that's that."

"But . . . Montes, that last day . . ."

"I know what Montes said. And I explained it to you. Those were just ravings. Montes is an artist. Anything could pop into his head. They're all just possibilities, thoughts. But that's it. I don't even want to think about what you must have imagined."

What I had imagined was that I didn't like any of that at all and that Helena was lying to me. I, in no way, believed that it was all as simple as she said it was, that Omar just decided to get out of the box early and that Montes had just left it at that. Although, on second thought, that was the most likely scenario. Anything else was too complicated. A murder, disposing of the body, cover ups, lies. It was too gruesome to be real.

"And why didn't you or Montes answer my calls?" I insisted.

"We're busy people," she said, somewhat annoyed. "Or do you by chance think that our entire world revolves around responding to your childish fantasies? People have to work, kid. And important people have things to do."

I didn't know how to respond. I sat staring fixedly at her, biting my tongue and clenching my fists in rage. She had hit a nerve. Kid? Important people? She had just told me that I was a nobody.

"Well I hope you know that this unimportant kid is going to go to the police right now, and then to the newspapers. And if you don't have anything to hide, then I'll be the one who looks stupid."

I don't know why, but that was the only response that occurred to me. And her expression changed radically. I sensed that she was more worried about the newspapers than the police.

"That's not what I meant, Marcos. I didn't mean to offend you. And there's no point in getting the police involved in this, much less the media. I don't think that will do any good for anybody."

"For anybody? Or . . . for you and Montes?"

"Come on, Marcos, calm down. There's no need to go to such lengths. I give you my word that nothing happened. It was all recorded. You can see it at the opening of the exhibition."

I noticed that her attitude was changing and starting to become conciliatory. Too much so, I thought.

"I'm truly sorry, Marcos, that it ended up like this between us."

"Like what?" I asked.

"Well, you know, with this tension. It isn't good . . ." she said, sitting down next to me on the sofa. "I would hate for it to stay like this. I've seen the way you look at me, Marcos. I'm not an idiot. Women know those sorts of things."

She slowly slid closer to me and, in her fragile and breathy voice, whispered in my ear:

"It's important, Marcos, that no one know anything about this. The work of art is the work of art, you understand, right?" I nodded, not knowing quite why I did so. "Marcos . . ." she said as she brought her mouth towards mine, "haven't you ever wanted to kiss me?"

I didn't respond. I had imagined that scene more than a hundred times. I had masturbated to the image of those shapely lips. And now I had them right there next to me, suggesting that I kiss them. But it was clear that it was nothing more than a trick. Helena was toying with me. It didn't take much intelligence to realize that. But even so, I didn't know what to do. I wanted to kiss her, to let myself do it, but there was something inside me preventing me from doing it. Rage and hatred. These feelings grew as I watched her toying with me, seducing me, without giving it a single thought, in order to keep me from saying anything.

I thought about Omar, about what Montes might have done to him. I thought about how Helena was revealing herself to be the very thing I had resisted accepting her as. And I was profoundly disgusted with all of it. Nevertheless, I couldn't help but notice the arousal I felt throughout my entire body. Helena was right there in front of me. And for a moment I thought that I also deserved to have my fantasies come true, even if this was the way it had to be done. What did anything else matter now?

Perhaps it did matter. A lot, most likely. But all of that was put on hold for the moment. And an absolutely strange feeling washed over me. A mixture of guilt and arousal that led me to succumb to Helena's charms, trying to pretend that she had truly seduced me.

I felt like that critical distance afforded me a certain amount of protection. I wanted to believe that I was the one who was really taking advantage of her, that I was only letting her believe that she was seducing me, when, in reality, I was in complete control.

As such, when my cock entered her mouth, I felt like my domination of her was total. She slid towards me, whispered my name in my ear, kissed me, and immediately put her hand on my crotch. When she realized that her actions had produced the desired effect, she pulled down my zipper with one hand and pulled out my cock, which was already hard, with the other. She put it in her mouth and passionately began to suck it.

I wanted to meet her gaze, but her hair was in the way. All I could see down there was a mass of hair compulsively moving back and forth. So I decided to close my eyes and enjoy it. But my pleasure was mixed with hatred. For some reason, I began to imagine that I was violently punishing her, forcing her to swallow all her words.

At some point, I forcefully grabbed her hair in my hand and pulled hard. With my other hand, I grabbed her throat and started to sink my fingers into her neck. Helena looked up at me for a few seconds, but kept on sucking, with increasing vigor and passion, as if that had turned her on. I felt like desire and rage were the same thing. I imagined Omar dying, Montes killing him, Helena lying about it. And I thought about the strange pleasure that aroused in me. I then recalled what Navarro had said: "Helena likes it rough." And right before I came, I choked her even harder—with all the strength I had—and held her head in place so I could ejaculate in her mouth. I wanted her to swallow it all. All the lies, all the frustration, all the pain that, wittingly or unwittingly, she had caused me. That's why I forced her to swallow my semen without coming up for air. That's why I choked her until my fingers hurt, until my fingernails sunk into her skin, until she started to gag on my cock and bit down on it hard.

I instantly screamed and kicked her away with my knee so hard that she fell to the floor. After a few seconds, without a word, she got up, came over to me and, wiping her mouth with her forearm, looked at me with an expression I was incapable of deciphering. Her face was purple, her eyes red. Her neck was completely crimson and a trickle of blood was running down her skin from the small scratches I'd made with my fingernails. And despite all that, the expression on her face was one of satisfaction. The origins of which were unknown to me. Perhaps she now understood what I was capable of. Or perhaps she was still just playacting.

I felt obscene and abject. I looked at her and couldn't open my mouth. Both of us remained silent for a few seconds. Then, without looking her in the eyes again, I put my cock back in my pants, zipped them up, and shot out of there without a word.

Only later did I have time to ponder what had happened. I wanted to believe that I had forced her to swallow her lies. But I soon realized that what she had really swallowed was my dignity. Perhaps that was the sole reason for her look of satisfaction.

V. MAGIC DOES NOT EXIST

1

After that night I tried to forget all of it. I needed to turn the page. The school year had ended. I'd received high honors in most of my courses. I'd graduated. There was nothing more for me to do in that city. So I decided to go back to my parents' house.

Back in the village, life was different. People sat out on the street at night in the summertime. Women played cards, and men played dominoes. For the first time, I started to take a certain interest in those scenes. We were fully in the twenty-first century, but there it seemed like a different era. I thought about the temporality of the city and of the immigrant neighborhood, and observed that clocks move at a different speed in each place. On a summer's night, time stood still. At least that's what happened on my street. I very rarely went out and took part in that stoppage of time, but I could see it from my window. And from there I could also listen as my mother tried to explain to the neighbors that I had graduated at the top of my class, but that that didn't guarantee anything and that I didn't know what I was going to do the following year.

"He says he's going to apply for a fellowship to get his doctorate and stay in school," she explained.

"Ah, young people. Nothing's ever enough for them," one of the neighbors said in reply.

"Well he likes being in school. Ever since he was little. It's in his blood," added another.

On more than one occasion, upon noticing that I was still in my bedroom, my mom said to me:

"Come on, Marcos, go outside and get some fresh air. You're going to get cooked alive in there."

And little by little I started to take a liking to going out on the sidewalk and reading novels. I'd sit near the women and, while they played sevens, I'd concentrate on my reading. Paradoxically, their chatter and laughter didn't bother me. What's more, for some reason, that background noise functioned as a wall of sound that protected me and made me forget everything I'd lived through in the weeks before.

However, when I was alone in my room, the images would come rushing back to me. It was all restored to my mind. And this restoration was reduced to the moment when I had choked Helena as hard as I could. It all led inexorably to that point. To my strange explosion of pleasure inside her mouth. There was nothing else. When I recalled it, the images came back to me, but also, and above all, the bodily sensations and the smells. I could smell my own semen and feel the viscosity of the liquid in the corners of Helena's mouth. I even thought about the time that I felt like I could smell Francisco's semen on Helena's mouth. And it all seemed to have some perverse meaning.

It was during that summer that I began to consider the possibility of writing down everything that had happened. That experience could make for a good novel someday. And if not a good one, at least a novel. So I started to get ideas for what might later become a book. I read a bunch of novels about the art world and I even started to try out a few methods of writing about my experience. I envisioned a structure that would open with the foreground shot of Bob Flanagan's penis and would end with me—or the protagonist of the novel, who, of course, would be a stand-in for me—ejaculating into Helena's mouth and choking her as hard as I could. It would be a vicious circle, literally. An insistent image and an obscene act. And, in between the two, a reality that was much more raw and obscene, that of a real world and a pretend world, that of a performance which, for some, was impossible to escape and a life which, for many others, was impossible to enter into entirely. It could be a novel about distance. About the necessary distance one must keep to be able to see things clearly, but also about the distance that must necessarily be abolished in order to experience those things. "Art and life." This was the issue I would attempt to consider. Because it was clear to me that the conjunction of the two could never be copulative. "Art and life" was an unthinkable connection. Copulation, literally, leads to life. Art or life. That was the great dilemma, and that was the question my book would try to consider. At those moments, I was convinced that I had chosen the latter option.

I spent my whole summer vacation trying to give shape to that story. I wrote hundreds of notes. I didn't have to use my imagination much. It had all really happened. It had happened to me. There was no need to bring in very much fiction. And, nevertheless, I couldn't find a way to write it in an organized manner. Perhaps it had to do with the distance, that distance that I hoped to discuss in the novel. A distance I lacked at that point. It had all happened too recently. It was all much too raw for me to be able to capture it in a book. And, above all, even though I didn't know it yet, the structure wasn't perfect. The book didn't end in Helena's mouth. The story wasn't over yet.

2

I received the bad news towards the end of August.

"Marcos, the artist, it's Ana. Do you remember me?"

"Of course," I said, although I was surprised she'd called.

"Sonia's dad . . ."—she hesitated for a moment—"died this afternoon."

I fell silent.

"She asked me to let her friends know. And you're the first one I called."

"But . . . how is she doing?"

"Well, you can imagine . . ."

The wake was going to be held at a funeral home on the outskirts of the city, near the university. Sonia had insisted that I didn't need to go. She didn't want to interrupt anyone's vacation. However, I didn't even have to think about it. I showered, changed my clothes, and in less than an hour I was on the road to the city.

I couldn't remember her dad's name, so when I got to the mortuary I gave Sonia's surname at the reception desk.

"Room four," said the receptionist.

It was my first time inside a funeral home. And I was surprised at how noisy it was. I had imagined that it would be completely silent, but what I actually encountered was a constant coming and going of people. An incessant murmur that transformed into a restrained silence when I entered the designated room, which was, nonetheless, completely packed, all the seats taken and a number of people standing against the walls. I stood in the doorway and timidly poked my head in to see if I could catch Sonia's eye. But I didn't see her anywhere. I spotted her mom standing in a corner of the room staring fixedly through a window, behind which, I assumed, was the body of the deceased. I was too embarrassed to go in and chose instead to remain outside, waiting for a chance to talk to Sonia. I sat down in the hallway to wait for her, not knowing exactly what I was going to say once I saw her. I had never been in that sort of situation, but I imagined that words weren't necessary.

While I waited for Sonia, I curiously observed everything going on around me. It obviously wasn't a joyful place, but it also wasn't as sad as I'd imagined. It seemed like a good place to be reunited with someone. The reason for it was terrible, it was the dead person who convened them all there, but at bottom it seemed like an affirmation of life. Hugs, memories, jokes . . . for a moment I understood why my dad and the other people back in the village had such a fondness for attending all the burials in the area.

After a few minutes, Sonia and Ana appeared in the hallway. I couldn't help but do a double take when I saw that they were holding hands.

"Oh, Marcos . . . you didn't have to come," she said, hugging me.

"Don't be silly . . ." I said. And I hugged her tight while tears welled up in my eyes. "I love you so much . . ."—I just blurted this out, almost without thinking. And I noticed that Ana, when she heard this, also started to cry. And upon seeing her cry, there was no way I could stop.

"There now, calm down, Marcos," said Sonia, emotional, but keeping it together. "Am I going to have to be the one consoling you?"

I don't know why it happened, but once I started to cry, there was no humanly possible way for me to stop. I didn't know Sonia's dad very well. But when I imagined for a few seconds the pain that Sonia must have been going through, I felt something break free inside me and I just let go.

"You're okay, come on now. And all this fuss on a day when I'm dressed in black just like you . . ." she said, laughing and drying her eyes at the same time. "You know something Marcos? Right before he died, my dad told me that he knew I was a lesbian and that I shouldn't worry, that he was fine with it. And he made me promise that I wouldn't hide it."

I looked at her in surprise.

"And that jokester made me promise that whenever I made a tortilla, it had to be the Spanish style tortilla, with potatoes and lots of onion. Can you believe it? Right up until the end, man, he had his sense of humor until the end."

"You've left me speechless. What did your mom say about it?"

"My mom? That I shouldn't break up with Ana and I should tell the rest of the world to go to hell."

Sonia went over to the doorway and said that she had to go in for a moment to be with her mother.

"I don't want to leave her alone for too long. Much less in the company of her crybaby cousins, who are just the worst. You two can stay out here."

She gave me another hug and went into the room. Ana stayed with me for a few minutes.

"That stuff about her dad is pretty powerful, right?" she whispered.

"Incredible."

"When she told me I just died . . . Oops, I'm sorry . . . I mean, I was really surprised." She cracked a smile. And, changing her tone of voice, said: "Well, what about your art piece? The opening is soon, right? I saw a poster for it the other day."

"Oh yeah?" I replied, surprised. I had disconnected myself from the matter so thoroughly that I'd forgotten the day of the opening was drawing near.

"Yep. There are signs for it at some of the bus stops. The image is really cool. It's a wooden box in the middle of a dark room. I like it. The title is . . . Jacobo Montes and . . . something else I can't remember. I don't know, something about escaping, I think."

"Well the thing is I ended up . . ."—I didn't quite know what to tell her—"I didn't end up getting along with Montes that well and I left the project."

"What a shame, because the exhibit is looking really sharp. That sucks. After all the work you put in." I nodded. "But . . . that's the way it goes sometimes. As a result, you learned about a lot of things you never knew existed. And, above all, you've realized you have an aptitude as an NGO volunteer that you'd never imagined you had," she said laughing. My smile was somewhat more forced.

Ana didn't wait too long to go back into the room to be with Sonia. I tried as best I could to avoid the possibility of going in and seeing the corpse. I had never seen a dead body and I didn't want that to change that afternoon. So I said goodbye to Ana and told her to give Sonia a hug for me. I'd see her the next day at the burial. I knew she wouldn't mind if I didn't go. But I really wanted to be there. Half an hour wasn't much of a sacrifice.

The church was overflowing with people and back where I was sitting you could barely hear what the priest was saying. He will be with Christ in heaven, we return to our true nature, the resurrection of the flesh . . . a series of clichés that, all the same, seemed to function in those moments as a balm to soothe the pain.

I recalled the funeral for Bob Flanagan, which appeared at the end of the Kirby Dick film. And I thought that what I was witnessing wasn't so different. It was all a theatrical representation that revolved around a real, incomprehensible, and unacceptable object: death. We were actually the audience of a grand performance. Death is the truest reality. But we look for any possible way to cover up that reality. The priest's eulogy, the ritual, the casket . . . methods of varnishing over that which is most dreadful. I then thought that, ultimately, they were all forms of iconostasis, means of keeping a distance from the inevitable. And it was clear to me that Montes's art intended to do the exact opposite of this, to remove that distance, to destroy the ritual, to arrive at that which is most real, even if it was never able to achieve it completely. Because the only real reality is death. The final border, the final obstacle. It is the place where everything ends. The most real, the most abject, the end of the performance. If Montes hoped to arrive at the real, death was the only solution.

I looked at the casket and couldn't help but think of the box that Omar had been shut in. There wasn't much difference. No one could escape from the box in front of my eyes at that moment. It was clear. What wasn't clear to me was whether it was possible to escape from the other box, the one that Montes used with Omar. Ultimately, I thought, Montes had performed magic. And Omar had disappeared. For me, as for the audience at a magic show, the trick had been successful. No one over here, no one over there. Omar had vanished. The way in which he had vanished was the thing that I had absolutely no way of knowing.

3

A large black sheet of canvas covered the façade of the Sala de Arte. "Jacobo Montes: Escape Attempt," written in silver lettering. The entrance was crowded, and it was almost impossible to get in. The entire art world had shown up to see the great socially engaged artist's exhibition.

I had gone back and forth a thousand times about going to the opening. It wasn't the best thing if I wanted to turn the page on all that. But, in the end, I couldn't help but go. My curiosity got the best of me, and I showed up with the intention of giving it a quick once-over and then heading back home. I in no way wanted to run into Montes or Helena again. I felt I had neither the strength nor the courage to come face to face with them.

As soon as I entered the space I noticed the smell. The unbearable stench of decomposition dominated the entire room. At that moment I understood why the majority of people there were in the doorway. I realized that the visitors were coming in, enduring it for a moment as best they could, and quickly leaving after seeing what was on display there. And what was on display was none other than the box, the same one in which Omar had been enclosed, which was now in the middle of the gallery, without any sort of pedestal, sharing space with the visitors, as if it were a minimalist sculpture. All of the lighting in the room was pointed at the wooden structure, leaving the rest of the space in shadows, in the darkness necessary to be able to see the two screens set up next to the box and little else. The first screen showed Omar entering the box and Montes closing it up a few seconds later. It was the scene that had been recorded in the warehouse, on a constant loop, which made it seem like there was an endless line of people getting into the box. The second screen showed a fixed shot, long and uncut, of the box. Just the box. Nothing more. I stayed in front of that screen long enough to see that no one got out of the box. I remembered that Helena had told me that Omar had eventually come out, that I'd see it for myself. But that moment never arrived. No one ever got out of the box. Strangely, that didn't surprise me. As soon as I'd seen the title of the exhibition and walked into the place, I intuited that the image of Omar getting out of the box wasn't going to be included among the pieces on display. Whether such an image actually existed or not, Montes certainly preferred to preserve the tension and toy with the spectators, making them think that no one had gotten out of the box, that it had been a failed escape, that it was all nothing more than a frustrated attempt to make an exit. And, from that starting point, the spectators could already draw their own conclusions.

In one corner of the room, which seemed almost to go unnoticed by most of the spectators, there was a small glass case next to a series of papers that were framed and hanging on the wall. I recognized it immediately: Omar's journal. The title was in Bambara, as were the pages, which were systematically displayed, some in the case and others on the wall. A grand, illegible archive that no one could understand. The few spectators who stopped in front of it looked at it with curiosity, but without knowing quite what they were looking at. Of course, as Montes had intended, it produced a sensation of perplexity and incomprehensibility.

No one knew what was in the box, no one understood what was written on the pages . . . no one knew anything about any of it. And, nevertheless, there everyone was, walking around it all, even though the stench was absolutely unbearable, even though it wasn't humanly possible to be in there without feeling nausea and revulsion. However, the spectators seemed to be propelled by some sort of masochistic urge, they insisted on enduring in front of the box, in front of the screen, next to the glass case, contemplating the papers hanging on the wall, withstanding the smell, steeling their stomachs, holding back their vomit . . . and all that without understanding any of it. I thought for a moment that what was happening there was a game of resistance similar to what Omar had been subjected to. A game governed by vanity and appearances. Whoever endured the longest in front of the work would be the one who understood it best, the one who had acquired the most symbolic and artistic capital, the one who was the most cultured, intelligent, and modern.

For a few seconds I thought about opening the box to show everyone what was hidden within. Although I wasn't exactly sure what I thought might be hidden inside. I assumed that Montes wouldn't have been so foolish, or so reckless, as to hide a corpse in there and risk his entire future in that way. It was all too obvious. The stench of decomposition, the idea of someone getting in the box, the closed box, and even the title of the work, *Escape Attempt*. Much too literal. Far too unsophisticated for Montes. Although, on the other hand, Montes's art had, as a matter of fact, always played with the obvious. Hiding something where everyone could see it would be his greatest success. In this case, all the evidence of a crime was right there. But it wouldn't occur to anyone to look inside the box. Nobody was going to desecrate a work of art. Ultimately, it was art. And art has its secrets and enigmas. We cannot hope to understand it entirely. Even when the thing to be understood is as real as can be, as close to us as possible, even when all distance has been eradicated . . . in the end, there is always an invisible barrier that separates the spectator from the thing she is looking at, in the end, what we see is always the very thing that is looking back at us, and in the end, nobody dares touch a thing. Because art is still sacred. And because nobody opens the sanctuary in the middle of mass to see if the body of Christ is really there, because nobody climbs up on stage to reveal the magician's secrets and expose what's behind all of his tricks. Because nobody dares to tear down the iconostasis. Because we fear that, if we were to do it, everything would vanish forever. Perhaps because, deep down, we're afraid that we would fade away if it were revealed that, in reality, nobody can just disappear as if by magic.

Magic. I thought to myself that art was nothing more than that. Magic, illusionism, pure prestidigitation. The artist was a magician, no longer an alchemist, as he had perhaps been in the past, but rather a prestidigitator, a swindler, and maybe a tightrope walker as well. Contemporary art wasn't that different from the circus or the fair. Perhaps this, and nothing else, was art's true affiliation: the cabinet of curiosities, the freak show, with the bearded woman, the strongman, and the magician. Art was the new "step right up and see." Even when there was nothing to see or when it was impossible to step right up.

I thought about all this as I stood in front of the box. And even knowing what I knew, intuiting what I intuited, I didn't dare tear down that distance and desecrate the sacred. I remained just like all the other spectators, wondering what was inside the box, what the secret hidden by Montes's art might be, how much of Omar's *Escape Attempt* was real and how much was fictional, whether all of that was art or life, or, better said, art or death.

And only one thing was clear to me: magic does not exist.

As I left the gallery I caught a glimpse of Montes. He was surrounded by politicians and people from the art world. He also saw me, and looked at me intently for a few seconds. His eyes contained the mystery that surrounded the box, the answers to all the unanswered questions I'd asked myself. I held his gaze, defiantly, trying to show him that I knew what he was hiding there, even though I actually didn't know anything and didn't even have the slightest idea of what had truly happened. He looked at me the way he had the time I saw his face in the reflection of the shop window on the day I first met him. I could almost hear the very words he'd said to me back then echoing in my head: "Soon we'll all be dead and will no longer sully the world." I still didn't understand it the second time around, but a shiver suddenly ran through my entire body.

Next to Montes, I saw Helena. She was wearing a scarf around her neck, right where the remnants of the small scratches from my fingernails probably were. She turned her head in my direction. I think she saw me. But in her case, I couldn't bear to meet her gaze. I lowered my head and got out of there as fast as I could. As I was leaving, I felt that I was also, in fact, carrying out my own escape attempt. And at that moment, I thought that perhaps I would never entirely know if some part of me would remain stranded in that place forever.

EPILOGUE

(A Novel, Not an Essay)

I left the city shortly thereafter. I was awarded a fellowship to pursue my doctorate in the United States and spent many years there. When I finished my dissertation, I returned to Spain and, in the end, paradoxically, got a job as a professor of contemporary art at the same university where I had been a student.

I never saw Montes or Helena again, although I did hear about them from time to time. He continued to work in the same vein of radical art, exploiting the disadvantaged social classes in order to make extreme situations visible. Little by little, his pieces started to fetch prices of the highest order and he ended up becoming one of the most expensive living artists. All the museums in the world were at his feet.

Helena spent two more years at the Sala de Arte, but in time she was offered a position as chief curator at an art foundation in Barcelona. From there, she took the leap to an art center in Rotterdam. After that, I lost track of her.

I resumed my life in the city. But I was still alone. Perhaps even more than before. Sonia and Ana had long since left town. And my parents had died while I was living abroad. I had my books and little more.

In the years leading up to that point, I never stopped writing texts about contemporary art and visual culture. Essays, art criticism, texts for catalogues, introductions, newspaper columns . . . But the book about Montes and his *Escape Attempt* always ended up getting pushed back for some other time. First the dissertation, then the classes I taught, then conferences, and, later on, art criticism and agreements to write all sorts of texts. I had tried to write the book on a number of occasions but I was never able to find the time to calmly reflect on those days and complete the project I'd started in my youth. However, it had never ceased to be a presence in my life, always lurking behind me, like background noise, like a constant murmur that, to greater or lesser success, I'd been able to keep quiet for all those years.

But everything changed in Paris. When I came across Montes's piece in the Centre Pompidou, the past rushed back with intensity, and I couldn't stop the background noise from coming to the surface. I realized then that, more than anything else, that box was full of memories that fought to be remembered once again. Beyond anything else that it might have really been hiding, the box also contained me, my life, my initiatory experience, as well as my distrust of art. And, for the first time in years, I felt that the time had come to stop and look back. Perhaps I was the one who had been attempting to escape all those years. And now the time had come to halt my escape and put everything in its proper place. Things relating to life and things relating to art as well.

I had written a lot during those years, of course, but I had never really pondered the ultimate meaning of what I was doing. After a period in which I had come to doubt everything, I ended up believing the lies. I had entered the art world and accepted its rules without further ado. I wrote, went through the motions, received money for the texts and conference presentations, but little else. I had become just another cog that helped the system function.

Ten years earlier, my experience with Montes had made me question everything for the first time and, for a while after, I had been convinced that art was just a grand fairy tale, a sham, and, above all, horribly immoral, a game for rich people and snobs that led absolutely nowhere. Nevertheless, over the years, that youthful impertinence, which I later considered pure naiveté, slowly lost its power until it faded away entirely.

But the box seemed to have brought it all back to me. The smell of rot emanating from the inside led me to think about the smell of rot in art generally. And I was certain that the true meaning of the art of the present existed in that box and that, in some way, art was something like the scene of a crime. But not of a perfect crime. Rather, this crime was overflowing with clues and spattered blood. A crime in plain sight, though no one ever picked up on the clues. Perhaps this was the only thing Montes was actually right about: "Art is a dirty thing, and there is no way to clean it without it losing its color."

Those were the contradictory sensations I experienced in Paris in front of Montes's piece that ended up motivating me to write the book once and for all. After thinking it over for a few days, I decided that perhaps this was the logical conclusion of my work from those years. I had devoted myself to writing about the poetics of blindness, the strategies of antivision, and the rhetoric of disillusionment. But what really seemed to be behind it all was Montes's box. My own theoretical work had been a strategy of occultation, with hidden noise. And the moment had arrived for me to recover my own story from the dustbin of history.

So I stopped writing the book I was supposed to be finishing up and started to write *Escape Attempt*. It would be all the same to the Ministry of Education and the grant I'd received. The only thing I had to prove was that I had been there writing. And if they ever questioned me about it, I could tell them that the novel was really the result of my research. And in fact it was, in some way. If not the result, then the conclusion. A conclusion that, paradoxically, had taken the form of a novel. Because the best way I found to give an account of those years and that process of disbelief in art was to narrate it all as if it were a novel. Of course, I was going to have to invent a lot of things. Names, places, situations, characters . . . but what I was interested in was conveying an experience, and I thought it was necessary to bend the truth so that the experience wouldn't disappear entirely. Sometimes a lie is more real than the truth.

That's why I decided to write a novel, not an essay. I imagined that it was a way to maintain a certain distance—distance, once again—and that I would put the things that the protagonist might do or say in someone else's mouth, even though the protagonist would ultimately be a stand-in for the author and many people still have trouble differentiating between character, narrator, and writer. That's why I decided to write a novel, not an essay. Because writing a novel allowed me to contradict myself. I could think one thing one day, and something completely different the next. I could discuss ideas that even I didn't understand entirely. But, above all, the novel format helped me put art and life together, to establish a connection between these two terms that were impossible to bind together.

My view of art, my trust or distrust, my theories, my way of seeing and experiencing it, depended a lot—entirely, I'd say—on my day-to-day life. And there was no barrier between the way I masturbated almost daily and the way I read, interpreted, and absorbed the institutional theory of George Dickie or the deconstruction of Jacque Derrida. And the novel, with all its conventions and clichés, could help me capture this continuum between life, thought, and writing. This was something that the essay was not yet prepared for. For some reason, I felt like I would adapt better to the conventions of the novel than those of the essay, that the novel was less rigid and that I could stretch it in ways that would tear the essay apart completely.

That's why I decided to write a novel, not an essay. Knowing, as well, that I was delving into territory that was totally foreign to me and into a different mode of writing, which would take me to places I'd never been before. I also knew that I was entering a no man's land and that the book would unavoidably end up weak in spots. But, even so, I decided to keep writing, with much greater difficulty when writing about my personal life than when writing about works of art, with a higher degree of artificiality when describing the protagonists of the novel than when musing about ideas or poetics. I didn't know how to avoid that bipolarity. Moments of reflection about art, allusions, ideas, and theories, as well as excessively quotidian, colloquial moments. Moments of speculation and meditation behind which one could sense years of experience in the profession, and moments of action that allowed one to sense the weaknesses of a novice writer. Moments of mature wisdom and moments of almost infantile naiveté. Any reader would be able to spot this disparity, and perhaps many would find it difficult to empathize with such irregularity. But I couldn't find a way to balance out that fluctuation. So I preferred just to let everything circulate between those two poles. And, at the time, it didn't matter that much to me. Because, ultimately, it made no difference to me what the result might be. The important thing was that the story had emerged once more and that, by writing it in this way, I felt like I could access a place that I couldn't reach when I was writing art criticism.

With these ideas in mind—and, for the first time in many years, with a certain amount of free time and tranquility—I wrote the book all in one go, over the course of my three-month stay in Paris, cooped up in a garret apartment on the campus of the Colegio de España. Three months, a period of time that, almost by chance, was the same length as the experience I was narrating. It was three months from the first time I heard Montes's name and the last time I saw him face-to-face. And three months is also how long it took me to write it.

Although the book had been gestating for years, in a way it had taken shape in real time.

Before making my return trip to the city, I printed out the result of my labor. When I saw the 230 printed pages and held them in my hands, I thought about how all of that was what lay behind a single piece by Montes. What lay behind, I said to myself. With varying degrees of success, I had managed to put it all into writing. And this invisible world that we never see in the artworks themselves, but which constitute them as such, was reflected in the book. Nonetheless, even after all that time spent thinking and writing, I still wasn't able to understand it all. There were many things that remained unclear to me. And they were still unclear to me because, ultimately, it all revolved around a void: I still didn't know what was in the box.

I thought that I should have been brave and opened the box on the night of the opening at the Sala de Arte, without worrying about what anyone else might have thought of me, taking the risk to desecrate the most sacred thing in the room. But I'd been a coward then, just as I was during the intervening years. And I was being a coward once again. My only act of bravery had been limited to writing Montes's story, declaring that art was a dangerous fairy tale and was just one more tool—perhaps the worst of them—of contemporary capitalism, that Montes was an abuser and his art, like a large portion of contemporary art, smelled of rot. My only act of bravery had consisted of writing that all of it had been corrupted and that none of it made sense. Everyone would be able to read about how I'd sold myself to the system and was now denouncing it at the top of my lungs, that I wrote for money, that I curated exhibitions I didn't like for money, that I didn't believe in the majority of things I wrote about, and that it was all a sham and much too late in the game to get out of it. Because I knew that, deep down, for as much as I'd written, for as much as I might publicly declare my cynicism, ultimately, sooner or later, I would go back to writing art criticism, giving conference papers on artists I wasn't interested in, traveling from one place to the next getting paid to legitimize, through my writings, a large number of idiocies, banalities, and horrible things made by inept, vile, and inconsequential artists.

I was thinking about all of this as I held the 230 pages of the book in my hands. That I had been a fraud the whole time for not saying what I thought and that I would probably continue to be a fraud after I returned home and got back to my routine, back to my classes, my writings, my conferences, and my exhibitions. I knew that everything wasn't going to change just because I'd decided to recount the whole story. I knew the book wasn't going to save me from anything, but there was no danger of it condemning me to anything either. At the end of the day, I had written a novel. And if things got ugly, I could always say that it was all made up, that I didn't really hold those ideas, and that what I'd written was nothing more than fiction. And that, like a good professional, I clearly knew how to differentiate between my position as a professor, essayist, and art critic and my attempt to become a novelist. If anyone ever asked me about it, I'd say that they were two completely different things and had nothing to do with each other, that I had written a novel about contemporary art in the same way as I could have written one about the invasion of an alien civilization. I would say that I'm not Marcos. At least not that Marcos. At least not in all respects. And there wouldn't be any problem. And that would only happen if someone from the art world actually managed to read what I'd written. Because I was still certain that nobody ever read anything, not even the critics, nor the artists, nor the curators, nor the journalists. It wouldn't even matter what I wrote. Nothing was going to change. Nobody was going to be convinced by one novel. It's been a long time since matters of art were decided by the writings of critics.

I was also certain that the book wouldn't be reviewed in the arts sections of the newspapers, that it would go completely unnoticed, and the whole endeavor would have been for naught. Perhaps the story only had significance during the time in which I wrote it, during the period in which I relived the past. But nothing more. Soon, everything would be back to normal. Ultimately, nothing is important. And it's necessary to escape everything. Escape from art, from the essay, from the novel, from all conventions. Escape . . . as Omar had once attempted to do.

Perhaps that's why, on the afternoon before I was set to leave Paris and return home, I went back to the Centre Pompidou and decided to do what I should have done from the start. I knew it was already too late. But for some reason I thought that, in this case, it was better late than never.

I went into the room and stood in front of the box for a few minutes, holding my breath as best I could. I waited until no one else was around. And that's when I did it. Only a few seconds passed between the moment I started to open the top of the box and the instant when the security guard, who must have been notified by walkie-talkie after someone saw what I was doing on the security camera, pounced on me and managed to immobilize me on the floor.

I didn't have much time, almost no time at all, actually, but even so I was able to catch a glimpse of the inside of the box. And then I saw it. The very thing I had always believed was there. The very thing I had always feared.

Nothing. Absolutely nothing. A big, dark emptiness. And at the bottom, a small container of liquid that seemed to be the source of the smell. I don't know what I expected to find. There was no way that Omar could have been in there. I sensed that. Or perhaps I even knew it. But I needed to see it with my own eyes. I needed to put my hand into the wound. No doubt about it, our era isn't one for believing without seeing.

There was nothing in there. And, nevertheless, right when the security guard yanked me backwards and away from the box, I was able to see some small scratch marks in the wood. As I fell to the floor,

I recalled *Night and Fog*, the Resnais film about concentration camps, and into my mind popped the image of scratch marks on the ceilings of the rooms where Jews had been gassed. They were the traces of barbarism, wounds in the concrete projected through history. I imagined Omar trying to scratch his way out of the box and Montes preventing him from escaping. And I once again thought about iconostasis, about who is saved and who is risking their life, and about how everything is ultimately a way to maintain a proper distance. Because this emptiness that was no longer an emptiness was nothing other than the sacred distance I had just desecrated.

As was to be expected, I had to pay a fine for vandalism. Two thousand euros, which I had no problem paying to the French government. A few newspapers reported on what I'd done. Some of them even suggested that it was a piece of performance art. However, as I'd once said to Montes in front of a shop window, I didn't have the slightest intention of becoming an artist.

A few weeks after the incident at the Pompidou, I received an e-mail from Montes that left me flabbergasted. He had found out about what happened and wanted to thank me for my collaboration on that piece. According to what he told me, he had been waiting for that moment for a long time. Up until that point, nobody had ever dared to do what I had done. At long last, the work had found its original meaning and had finally been activated. Finally, someone had done something. Something that, nevertheless, demonstrates that actions cannot change things. Because, in the end, things are nothing but mere empty appearances.

The e-mail went on to say that, after the controversy, the Centre Pompidou had decided to put on a large-scale retrospective of his work and that he would like me to write something for the exhibition. It seemed he had been following my work from a distance. He had read all my writings and had always believed that one day I would write a great book about him. But it wasn't until after my performance in Paris that he really felt like the right moment had arrived.

Money was no object. The museum was willing to pay me whatever was necessary. And they also didn't care what form the text took. I had absolute freedom. He said that he had read some text of mine that flirted with the boundaries between genres and that he'd liked it. So I could write whatever I wanted to. Even a novel, if I so pleased. The important thing was for a book of mine to accompany the exhibition.

I didn't respond for a few days. I had to think about it. His e-mail had completely thrown me for a loop, and I didn't know how to react. There was a lot of money at play. It was a great museum. And the exhibition was, without a doubt, going to be one of the most important artistic events of the year. It was the opportunity I had been looking for to establish myself as an important art critic. What's more, I had already done the work. The novel was already written. I'd just have to touch it up a little, although not that much. But that was the least of it. I didn't care about the money. Or the fame. The only thing that interested me was that perhaps my novel would finally be able to make a few things clear. That it would tell the world who Montes was and what art was.

I didn't have to think about it much to realize my mistake. If I wrote about Montes in the context of that exhibition, he would always come out on top, as had happened with the box. Whatever I wrote, it would legitimize his actions and thus degrade Omar and everyone else even more. On that playing field, Montes always had the advantage. Art always wins inside the art world. And outside of it, no one would listen. So I was trapped. Say it from the outside and ensure it would never be heard, or say it from the inside and run the risk of being manipulated.

That's why in the end I refused to do it. Sooner or later I would surely end up writing art criticism again and I'd continue to fall in line just like everyone else. I'd go back to curating exhibitions, giving conference presentations on art, writing catalogues, legitimizing all sorts of nonsense and banality that I didn't believe in. I would certainly return to art at some point. But not now, not at this moment, not with Montes. At least this one time I would try to maintain my dignity. It wasn't much. Almost nothing. But it was at least something. Just like the e-mail I finally sent him. Brief and concise: I would prefer not to.

This book was written to mark the occasion of the exhibition *Escape Attempt: Jacobo Montes and the Ethics of Distance*, on display at the Centre Georges Pompidou between February 13th and May 15th of 2013. The author would like to thank Helena Román, the museum curator, for her collaboration and involvement with this project. Similarly, the author would like to state explicitly his profound appreciation of the Jacobo Montes Foundation, which enabled him to spend three months in Paris to write this book.

ABOUT THE AUTHOR

Miguel Ángel Hernández Navarro (Murcia, Spain, 1977) is Associate Professor of Art History at University of Murcia and was formerly the director of the Centro de Documentación y Estudios Avanzados de Arte Contemporáneo (CENDEAC). He focuses on antivisual art, contemporary art theory, migratory aesthetics and memory. He is author of several books on art and visual culture.

As a fiction writer he has written a journal, a book of short stories and the novel Escape Attempt, shortlisted in the Premio Herralde de novela, and which has been translated into French, German, Italian, and Portuguese as well as English. He is currently a fellow of the Society for the Humanities at Cornell University.

ABOUT THE TRANSLATOR

Rhett McNeil is a scholar, critic, and literary translator from Texas, where he graduated Phi Beta Kappa from UT-Austin with degrees in English, Portuguese, and Art History. He has an MA in Comparative Literature from Penn State University and is currently finishing a PhD in the same department, with a doctoral minor in Aesthetics. While at Penn State, he has taught courses in comparative literature, film, Spanish, and Portuguese. His translations include novels and short stories from some of the most innovative and accomplished authors on the world literary scene, including Antônio Lobo Antunes, Enrique Vila-Matas, Gonçalo M. Tavares, João Almino, and A.G. Porta. Rhett also edited and translated a volume of short fiction by the Brazilian master Machado de Assis, who, along with Jorge Luis Borges, is the subject of his dissertation. His translation of Tavares's Joseph Walser's Machine was longlisted for the 2013 Best Translated Book Award.

Lightning Source UK Ltd.
Milton Keynes UK
UKOW01f0912100416

271900UK00003B/44/P

9 788494 365874